The SWAT team approached, advancing from parked car to parked car, weapons ready. They were about a block from the wreckage when the front passenger door of the upended truck flipped open and demons began to climb out and down to the street.

The SWAT team opened fire on the demons. Some fired back as they continued to clamber out and flee.

Paige counted as they climbed out, ducking as shots were fired, then looking back up. "Six . . . seven . . . eight . . ." She glanced at Phoebe. "Four went in, eight came out."

Charmed®

Published by Simon & Schuster

DEMON
DOPPELGANGERS

An original novel by Greg Elliot

Based on the hit TV series created by

Constance M. Burge

SIMON SPOTLIGHT ENTERTAINMENT
New York London Toronto Sydney

This book is a work of fiction. Any references to historical events, real people, or real locales are used fictitiously. Other names, characters, places, and incidents are the product of the author's imagination, and any resemblance to actual events or locales or persons, living or dead, is entirely coincidental.

S|S|E

SIMON SPOTLIGHT ENTERTAINMENT
An imprint of Simon & Schuster Children's Publishing Division
1230 Avenue of the Americas, New York, New York 10020
® & © 2005 Spelling Television Inc. All Rights Reserved.
All rights reserved, including the right of reproduction in whole or in part in any form.
SIMON SPOTLIGHT ENTERTAINMENT and related logo are trademarks of Simon & Schuster, Inc.
Manufactured in the United States of America
First Edition 10 9 8 7 6 5 4 3 2 1
Library of Congress Control Number 2005925958
ISBN-13: 978-1-4169-0026-9
ISBN-10: 1-4169-0026-8

For my daughter, Katie, who keeps me young

Chapter One

Paige Matthews orbed herself and her nephew, Wyatt, to the north edge of Lincoln Park, materializing in a small thicket at Land's End. She quickly checked to see if anyone was around who could have seen her, although she knew the chances of that were slim. It was Tuesday, June 21, the first morning of summer, but the blustery conditions were decidedly unsummerlike, and she was convinced the weather would keep most people from a location this open to the elements.

Confirming that they were alone, she checked on Wyatt, making sure he was bundled against the wind. Then she pushed the baby stroller out of the woods and into the open.

"I love coming here," she said to the baby, "and I thought today would be a good day to share it with you, too."

She always talked to Wyatt as if he could understand her every word, and she sometimes

1

wondered if he could, in fact, do just that. He seemed to understand his parents, Piper and Leo, far more than other babies could understand theirs. That, of course, was because, like Paige, he was the product of a witch and her Whitelighter, her guardian. To Paige, this created a special bond between Wyatt and her, and it was part of the reason she'd brought him here today, part of the reason she talked to him as if he were an adult rather than just a baby.

She pushed the stroller near the edge of Land's End and stopped, taking in the view: the sweep of the Presidio, with its hills and trees curving away from the park and stretching to the Golden Gate Bridge; the bridge itself, holding its mass above the expanse of water on spires lifting heavenward; and the bodies of water separated by the bridge, the enclosed bay on one side surrounded by the city, the open ocean on the other, the home of the elements. The wind blustered enough to keep the bridge in view, making the whole panorama breathtaking.

Paige took it in for a moment silently, smelling the salt air, then continued her conversation with Wyatt. "Do you see that?" She checked to ensure that he in fact could see the view, that he was still bundled against the wind and the cold. Then she straightened, continuing her explanation. "That, over there, is the Pacific." She pointed out over the gray ocean, its white-topped waves falling over one another as the wind pushed them under the bridge and into San Francisco Bay. "That landmass, the one with all the trees and not much in the way of buildings, is the Presidio. And that"—here she pointed to the bridge itself—"is the Gate. Nice name, don't you think?" She smiled, repeating it. "The Gate. The pathway from one life to another. From the wild of the sea to the civilized world, to all that humankind has built."

She paused. "It's like a metaphor for you and me, Wyatt. The place where nature and things beyond humankind's control meet the world as we know it." She breathed deeply, closing her eyes. "And today, it's summer. You may be dressed like it's still winter, but it's really summer." She smiled again. "That ol' summer will come on its own terms, not ours."

She took in the view for a moment longer, then turned the stroller. "Okay, enough of this. Let's get out of this wind and see the rest of the park."

She pushed the stroller toward the Legion of Honor Museum. "I wonder what's happening at the museum today," she said. "Maybe Auntie Paige can show you some antiquities." She stopped as a tour bus rolled up to the front entrance of the museum. "Oh, look, Wyatt, tourists. Let's see how many of them think that just because it's summer, it'll be hot enough for shorts and T-shirts."

As the bus disgorged its passengers, Paige

noted that there were indeed several dressed in shorts, or in other clothing too light for the day's chilly conditions. She watched as they hurried into the museum, hugging their cameras as if for warmth.

"See that?" she asked Wyatt. "Those tourists are another metaphor, in their own way." She glanced down to see if Wyatt was watching them. "They come to California expecting sunshine, blue skies, palm trees, and balmy breezes. They watch too much TV." She looked at the tourists scurrying for the doors of the museum, most of them rushing right past the huge statue, Rodin's *Thinker*. "They don't know what effect that ocean, with its invisible currents, has on our weather. Just like they have no idea how the forces of *our* world, the world of magic, affect life here for them, for the ordinary people."

She was about to continue when one young man stepped off the bus, nearly the last to do so. He, too, was dressed in jeans and a T-shirt, but he was smiling. He turned to the bay, breathed deeply, and—instead of hurrying into the museum like the rest of the tourists—walked toward the ocean.

Paige retreated a bit into the brush, watching this handsome young man, so surprised by his actions that she let her last sarcastic quip die on the tip of her tongue.

The young man moved to a low-lying rock, very near to where Paige stood with the stroller, and climbed up on it. Facing the ocean, he removed his shirt and spread his arms out wide, seeming to embrace the chill wind that bore down on him.

Paige noted that he looked even more handsome with his shirt off.

Wyatt squealed out what sounded very much like a laugh, and the young man jumped at the sound. He turned, spotted Paige, and quickly put his shirt back on. "Sorry," he said. "I didn't mean to disturb you and your baby, ma'am."

"Don't worry, you didn't. And just for the record, I'm his aunt, not his mom." Paige moved the stroller closer to the stranger, who had by now hopped off the rock. "So, what were you doing there?" she asked.

"Oh, just kind of . . ." He looked back out at the ocean. "It's so big, you know? So powerful." He smiled sheepishly. "I'm from Kansas. We don't have an ocean there. So to be this close, to be here—" He broke off, shaking his head. "I'm sure it sounds loony, but I just wanted to, you know, greet the ocean. On its own terms. To acknowledge all that power."

Paige nodded, impressed, perhaps even stunned, that a tourist could be awed by the same power that she'd come here to introduce to Wyatt. "I see," she managed. For a moment she shared a look of understanding with the young man.

"Well," he said, "I'd better catch up with my tour."

"Enjoy the museum," she said. "And the ocean."

"Thanks. I intend to."

Paige watched as the young man turned and walked away. She noted that he walked faster on his way to the museum, like the other tourists had. But he stopped to admire the Rodin. Just before moving toward the entrance, he looked back, spotted Paige still watching him, and smiled. Then he disappeared into the museum.

"Well," Paige said to herself as much as to Wyatt, "that was certainly interesting." She glanced at the baby. "I know, I know, I shouldn't lump all tourists into one basket, right? Because as soon as I do, one will surprise me." She rolled the stroller closer to the museum, past the bus, past the sculpture garden, and nearer the entrance. "Don't worry," she said, "I'm not planning on hanging around just for another peek at Mr. Young and Handsome. Besides, he'll be on his way back to Kansas soon."

Wyatt burbled, this time sounding like "Ohhh," and he pointed with his little fingers at the large banner rustling in the wind over the entrance to the museum.

"What's that, Wyatt?" She read the banner. "Oh. Greek antiquities. A touring exhibit, arriving soon." She smiled. "We should come back for that show. Auntie Paige actually knows quite a bit about Greek antiquities. I could probably even . . ." She stopped, turning this new idea over. "Let's go home, Wyatt. Let's tell Mommy all about our day."

"Sounds like you two had fun," said Piper Halliwell. She sat in front of Wyatt, now in his high chair, feeding him as Paige told her about their adventure. "I hope Wyatt here didn't cramp your style with that buffed-out guy."

"No, of course not." Paige regarded her sister, enjoying the warmth of the kitchen, the smell of baking bread. "And that's not why I went back to the entrance. Not the only reason, anyway."

"Greek antiquities, right. Sounds interesting. Maybe we could all go."

"I'm not just talking about going to see it," Paige explained. "I want to get a job there."

Piper cocked an eyebrow. "Really?"

"Yeah. As a tour guide or something. Just for the time that the exhibit is in town."

"It sounds perfect for you. You know a lot about Greek art, Greek history. More than most people. Just don't go running off to the next city on the tour with some Greek god."

"I promise." Paige smiled and walked to the phone. She dialed the museum's number and made her pitch.

Later that afternoon Piper walked into P3 with Wyatt on her hip. "See how quiet it is at this time of day?" She touched him on his button nose.

"So we won't bother anyone, and no one will bother us." She headed for her office.

She'd just settled Wyatt into the corner with some baby toys when her cell phone rang. She glanced at the number. "Look, Wyatt, it's Aunt Phoebe." She snapped the phone open. "Hey, Phoebes, what's up?"

"I need a favor. Can you see if I left a folder of letters to be answered in the bathroom?"

"Gee, I'd love to," said Piper, "but I'm not at home. I'm at the office."

"That explains why you're not picking up the land line." There was a short pause. "What are you doing there this time of day?"

"Checking inventory."

"Umm . . . don't you have someone who does that for you?"

"Usually," said Piper, "but there's a discrepancy in the numbers. It looks like we've been short a bottle of premium tequila on every order this month. Same brand every time. And it's the most expensive one we carry."

"So you think . . ."

"Yes," said Piper. "I'm worried that someone is selling it off the books and keeping the cash for themselves."

"Bummer. How will you find out?"

"I'm going over the books myself while it's quiet here."

Wyatt giggled from the corner.

"You've got Wyatt with you?" Phoebe asked.

"Yeah. He's happy putting toys in his mouth. And I really didn't want to be down here all day, so when he gets tired of it, it'll be time to head home."

"Good luck tracking that discrepancy down," said Phoebe.

"Yeah." Piper sounded glum. "I'm really hoping I don't have to fire anybody. I like the staff. And until now, I trusted them."

"Just remember that the most obvious answer usually *is* the right one."

"Gee," said Piper, "that sounds an awful lot like an 'Ask Phoebe' platitude."

"Does it?" Phoebe stopped a moment. "Sorry. I guess it does."

"Don't worry about it." Piper opened the accounting books on her desk. "Listen, I'm going to get at this. I'll see you back at the Manor." She hung up, sighed, and began crunching numbers.

Paige sat in the museum office across the desk from the woman, waiting. She thought the woman looked perfect for her job. Poised, cultured, with her own classic beauty, she could have been a Greek goddess herself. The nameplate on her desk read GRACE STEPHENS.

Ms. Stephens read the paper in her hand. "Impressive. Most of our applicants know the Titans, of course, but it's nice to see that you have a grasp of the mythological gods who came before them. Chaos, Gaea, Eros . . . you've got them all pegged." She turned the page over. "And you apparently know as much about Greek architecture as you do about mythology. I especially like your description of the temples of Athena and Apollo. You're able to convey what's important about them in your own words, so it doesn't sound like you did your research online last night." She looked up. "Which is exactly the quality we want for this job, that ability to take the ancient and make it sound current, alive, rather than like some stodgy, musty old relic."

Paige smiled. "So, how long before I know . . ."

"Oh. You're hired. Sorry, did I not make that clear? I'd like you to take the catalog home, study it, do your own research on any items that you aren't familiar with, and come back here next Monday at nine. I'll walk you and the other new hires through the exhibit before the opening on Tuesday."

Paige rose, thrilled. "Thanks very much, Ms. Stephens."

Grace held out her hand. "Welcome to the museum."

Paige left the office, glancing about at the museum that would soon be her workplace, taking in the smells of antiquity—and that's when she saw him. The young man from that morning, coming out of the office next to Grace's. Clad now in a pair of slacks and a dress shirt, he looked much less touristy, but just as handsome.

Paige stepped back, uncertain, and let him pass without his seeing her.

There were few coincidences in the lives of the Charmed Ones, she knew. She wondered what role this young man was to play in her future.

Chapter Two

Paige walked into Halliwell Manor, conscious of its warmth, its smells. Simmering spaghetti sauce this time. She stood in the kitchen, absently tearing off a piece of a baguette Piper had baked that morning, dipping it into the sauce.

"Piper will kill you. That sauce is hours away from being done."

Paige turned to see Phoebe standing in the doorway to the kitchen. "Speaking of Piper, where is she?"

"P3," Phoebe answered. "Inventory."

"Oh." Paige frowned. "And what are you doing home this time of day?"

"I came back for this." Phoebe held up the folder of letters.

"Phoebes? Why does the ink on that folder look so . . . waterlogged?"

"Oh. That." Phoebe shrugged. "I was reading letters in the bathtub."

"Because . . . ?"

"Because that's the way Abby and Ann did it. And you know what? I can see why." She sat down. "You know that place you can get to in the tub? That Zen kind of place, where your thoughts are clear?"

"I guess. I'm more of a shower person."

"Same thing. But you can't read letters in the shower. Anyway, I tried it, and wrote some responses that I thought were pretty good, then went off and left the whole folder on the bathroom floor."

"Where it got dripped on?"

"Yeah. But I can still read it. Most of it." She opened the folder. "I checked. See?" Phoebe held up the folder. She studied Paige's face as she sat across from her, and grew concerned. "Oh, you didn't get the job. Sorry."

"No. I *did* get it. Six weeks of walking tourists through the coolest collection of Greek artifacts I've ever seen."

Phoebe reacted, surprised. "Paige! That's . . . great! But why do you look so . . ."

"Have you got a minute?"

Phoebe glanced at her watch and lied. "Sure."

Paige told Phoebe the whole story: the walk with Wyatt, the encounter with Young and Handsome, the idea that somehow this tourist understood more than most about the powers of the world, and the second, unexpected sighting of him at the museum.

"You're right," Phoebe agreed. "This is likely not a coincidence. But why duck him? Why not say hello?"

"Because I don't know what it means."

"Paige . . . ," Phoebe selected her words carefully. "Okay, granted, the universe has plopped this guy down in front of you. Twice. But you can't back away from that. You can't keep avoiding him. If you do, how will you ever find out why he's been put in your path?" She watched her sister's face. "And don't worry so much. For all you know, he's just somebody you're supposed to date."

"He's a tourist. He's probably gone by now."

"Maybe, maybe not." Phoebe stood. "Listen, I've got a deadline, and I still have to type these up." She closed the folder. "But watch for this guy. Something tells me he's not out of your life yet." She leaned over the stove, sampling the forbidden sauce herself. She nodded her approval of the sauce, wiped her lips, and turned back to her sister. "And if you do see him again, grab him. By the forelock, if you have to."

Paige smiled. "That sounds like something you'd say in 'Ask Phoebe.'"

"Does it?" Phoebe stopped, uncertain. "Do I really do that?"

"It's okay," said Paige. "I think you're right. So if I see him again, I won't miss another opportunity."

• • •

Monday morning Paige walked up the steps of the museum, her heart beating fast. She'd spent the week poring over the exhibit's catalog, researching every item online, connecting it to a place, a time, an event. The Peloponnesian War. The early Olympics. The Spartan lifestyle.

She was ready.

Grace stood at the door of the conference room, welcoming those who entered. "Paige," she said. "Come in."

Paige entered the room and was surprised that there were so many people there. Sixteen new guides, hired for one tour.

"Thank you all for being so prompt," Grace began, closing the door and walking to a desk. "I think that's everyone except—"

The door opened and Young and Handsome strode in, glancing sheepishly at Grace. "Sorry, am I late?"

"No, no. Right on time. Sit down."

Paige felt herself flush. He was here. Again. And the only empty seat was the one next to her. Y&H walked over, nodded politely to her, and sat, looking up expectantly at Grace, waiting.

"All right, I trust you all have had time to go over the catalog. Any questions?"

A young woman seated in the back row asked Grace about the coins on display. As Grace answered, Y&H turned back to Paige, recognition slowly spreading over his features. "Hey. I remember you . . . Auntie."

Paige gave him a tight-lipped smile. "That's me."

He started to say something more, but Grace interrupted. "I want us all to have time to get to know one another at lunch. Right, now, if there are no more questions for the moment, let's begin your first tour."

Paige walked through the exhibit awkwardly, as if she'd forgotten how to move. She tried to concentrate, commented on a piece she'd studied—her remark suddenly sounded stiff and wooden—and worked to ignore Y&H, who seemed perfectly capable of standing next to her for most of the tour while ignoring her completely.

Finally, it was lunchtime. She sat in the museum café, waiting. Y&H got his food and sat one table over from her. He faced the terrace, which overlooked the ocean, and seemed lost in the view. She watched him, examined his face, noticed that he did, indeed, have a forelock. A soft, light brown one, drifting impishly into the middle of his forehead. She resisted the urge to grab it. But, she decided, it was time to seize the moment, if not the hair. She got up and moved so she stood next to him, trying to look as if she'd just walked up with her sandwich.

"Still in love with the ocean, I see."

He looked up, smiled, and nodded, looking back at the view.

She waited.

He looked back to her again. "Sorry. Would you like to sit down?"

"Thanks." He wasn't making this easy.

She worked to relax, watching the ocean as well. This wasn't so tough. She could do this. "Tell me what you see," she said.

He continued to watch for a moment. "I don't think it's what I see as much as what I feel when I look out there."

She liked that. "Okay, tell me what you feel."

"This is probably going to sound weird, but last week—that day you saw me doing the ministriptease on that rock—that was the first time I'd seen the ocean. Really seen it. Not a glimpse from the bus while we're coming from the airport, but really, actually, been in . . . its presence." He looked over. "I'm probably freaking you out right now, talking like some crazy—"

"No," she interrupted. "No, you're not. I get it."

"Anyway, when I saw it, I knew I had to stay. For a while, at least. So I forgot about going back to Kansas, and when I saw that notice here in the museum that they were hiring—"

"There was a notice?"

"Yeah." He looked at her curiously. "Isn't that how you knew about the job?"

"No. I just called."

"Huh." He let this go. "Anyway, I saw that as fate, sort of. I wanted to stay, I wanted a job that was as close as I could get to that view, and there was one right here." He lowered his voice. "I don't know much about Greek antiquities. I wouldn't know a Greek statue from a Roman one. I just wanted to be near where I'd first felt the power of that ocean."

"But . . . the test . . ."

"I sort of cheated on that."

"Oh."

"Yeah. That guy who gave me the test just left me in his office, and there was this stack of other people's tests right there. . . ."

"The interview. You managed to fake that, too?"

"I went through college on an athletic scholarship. And I sort of, um . . . I sort of picked up the art of impressing people while at the same time not having the slightest idea what I'm talking about."

"I see." Her grip on his forelock seemed to be loosening. She considered crossing him off her list of guys who were dating material. Still, he *was* easy to talk to, to look at, and he did have that abiding attraction to the ocean's power. "So, after you got the job . . . you didn't study the catalog?"

"I did. But I also went to Alcatraz, rode the trolley cars. You know . . . I was a tourist."

"And when Ms. Stephens figures out you don't know a Doric column from an Ionic from a Corinthian?"

"Now that, I know. Basically, it's plain,

fancier, fanciest." He looked at her with his clear green eyes. "But you've got to know that most people on any tour we give will be bored to death if we stop to give them any more of an explanation than that."

Paige wondered if he was right, if she was about to turn into the kind of tour guide who bored everyone to tears. She hoped people weren't really as uninterested as he'd just made them out to be.

"So . . . ," he continued.

Those eyes brought her around again.

"You really know about this Greek stuff?"

"I do, yeah."

He pulled out his catalog. "Just so I don't get fired on my very first day, could you . . . ?"

"Sure." She looked at the catalog, at the items listed there, and decided to lay out the simplest, most basic version of the information. "Let's start with those statues."

The rest of the lunch hour flew by. Paige was aware of how close he was, how those warm, beautiful eyes lit up when he got what she was saying. She used those eyes as her guide: When they lit up, she went further into her explanation. When they grew restless, she moved on. He became her test subject for when she was giving too much detail. She remembered what he'd said about the columns.

"You two must be the most studious new hires we have."

Paige looked up to see Grace standing beside her.

Grace went on. "And while I must say I admire your focus, the rest of us have moved back into the exhibit."

"Oh." Paige felt herself blushing. "Sorry."

"This way." Grace turned and walked out of the café.

Y&H looked sheepishly at Paige. "Guess we should join her, huh?"

"Yeah. Maybe this isn't the best time to have a cram session." Paige rose, picking up her catalog.

"So, what *would* be the best time?"

Paige turned, regarded him, and thought again about his forelock. She reached down and scribbled her name and phone number on the front page of his exhibit pamphlet. "Call me. We'll find a time."

"Thanks. I will."

"And when you call, how will I know it's you?"

He looked at her blankly for a moment. Then it hit him. He laughed softly at himself. "Sorry. My name's Chase."

"Chase," she repeated. She liked the way she felt when she said it. "Call me, Chase."

She turned, her face burning with a different kind of flush, and followed Ms. Stephens back into the galleries.

Chapter Three

Piper came into the Manor, Wyatt once again riding her hip like a baby koala.

"Oh, good," said Phoebe, "you're home. Dinner's ready."

Piper sat Wyatt down in his playpen and turned to Phoebe. "*You* made dinner?"

"Between you spending every afternoon this week at P3 and Paige always at the museum or the library or some coffee shop with what's-his-name, I figured I'd better pitch in."

Piper breathed in, following her nose toward the kitchen. "Smells like . . . pizza?"

"It is," said Phoebe. "The best pizza money can buy."

Piper turned at the kitchen door. "I thought you said—"

"I didn't say I was cooking. I said I pitched in." Phoebe changed the subject as she followed Piper into the kitchen. "So, how are P3's books?"

Piper made a noise in her throat like a strangled animal. "Still driving me crazy," she said. "If I haven't solved this by the end of the week, I'm hiring an independent accountant."

"Um, won't that cost more than a few bottles of premium tequila?"

"*Way* more." Piper opened the pizza box and began cutting slices. "But I have to find the answer or this is going to mess up the books forever." She put slices onto plates. "I finally called a meeting of the staff today and told them what I suspect. I made it clear that the guilty party can tell me now and I'll let them off pretty easy. But if I have to find them on my own, heads won't just roll, they'll fly out the door." Piper noticed the look on Phoebe's face. "What, that isn't the way 'Ask Phoebe' would handle it?"

Before Phoebe could answer, Leo walked in. "Thought I smelled pizza," he said.

Piper gave him a kiss. "Hey," she said. She handed him a plate. "Here." She turned back to Phoebe. "So, where *is* Paige tonight?"

Paige leaned on her elbows at the table, her hands feeling the warmth from her coffee cup as they wrapped around its ceramic circumference. She realized that as long as Chase was talking, she could stare into his eyes all she wanted to and get away with it.

He was talking a lot.

"I've got to tell you," he said, "it's the engineering that I can't get over. They built buildings and temples that are *so* artful, you know? And built them so well that they're still here twenty-five hundred years later. It's awesome."

Paige, feeling suddenly as if she needed to contribute, nodded. She wanted him to keep talking.

He did. "It was those columns that got me started. Remember? You made a comment that I should know more about them that first day at the museum."

Paige was caught off guard. "I don't think that's what I meant."

"Doesn't matter. You said it, so I did it." He stared at her, cocking his head. "Did you know that the first columns, the Doric ones, were designed after the human form? They measured some guy's foot, then measured how tall he was, and saw that the ratio was one to six. So they decided that the columns should be the same ratio, so it would look like men were holding up all those temples."

"I did know that," she said.

"But then," he went on, still charged up, "they made the Ionic columns more slender, like a woman is."

"Yeah."

"And then," he said, his hands sliding across the table toward hers, "they made the Corinthian columns even more beautiful. Because they'd figured out that you women are so much better looking than us guys are."

Paige held his gaze until she realized he wasn't talking anymore, then looked down, feeling the urge to reach her hands toward his as well. She fought that urge. "So," she said, looking back up, "you said you found something else you needed my help with?"

"Yeah." His hands retreated, and he opened the file in front of him, reading what was there, giving Paige the chance to stare at him again. "It's about the armaments we have in the display," he said. "I've been studying Greek warfare and I was looking for some specifics so I could talk more about the swords and spears and shields when I'm doing my tours. I wondered if I could ask you a few things that I can't find online."

"Sure," said Paige. She glanced around. The coffee shop was nearly deserted. If she was going to make a PDA, a public display of affection, this wouldn't be a bad place, or a bad time. When she looked back at Chase, he glanced up at her and smiled.

The urge to take his face in her hands and kiss it was almost overwhelming. But she had her reasons to be cautious. "Go ahead, ask away," she said.

The next day Phoebe stood in the doorway of her newspaper office, the sounds of dozens of keyboards clacking in the background. She watched Paige, who sat at Phoebe's desk, for only a moment before speaking. "What are you doing?"

Paige turned, surprised. "Oh, hi. Guess you're back from lunch, huh?"

"Is something wrong with your laptop?"

"No." Paige indicated Phoebe's computer. "It's just that your screen is so much bigger, the resolution is better, and your T-3 connection is *so* much faster than my download speed."

Phoebe walked closer, examining the Greek armor on the computer screen. "Speaking of speed, I thought you were up to speed on all the Greek artifacts."

"Yeah, pretty much. But Chase has taken a real interest in the warfare display. He was telling me all about this one sword he saw online that the museum doesn't have. He says it has Medusa on one side of the hilt and Pegasus on the other. Turns out those are only on modern replicas."

"So you're going to set him straight?"

"I can't have him mouthing off to his tours about cool Greek swords made last year in Detroit."

"You're *still* tutoring him?"

"Not so much tutoring anymore," Paige said. "The first week, sure, that's what it was. But this week, it's more like we're exchanging notes. He's studying a lot on his own. He's really into the battlefield strategies of the Greeks. I heard him on one of his tours. He's not half bad."

"Thanks to you."

"In part, I guess."

Phoebe leaned against the edge of her desk. "You think this could turn into a relationship?"

Paige sighed as she glanced up at her sister, then looked back to the screen. "Too soon to tell. I mean, he's hot. That hair, those eyes, that bod . . . and we get along. He's really pretty smart, when he decides to put his mind to something. But I'm still making up my mind about him."

"That's what you keep telling us. And yet, it seems like you've spent every waking minute of the last two weeks either at the museum or at some beachside coffee shop filling his head with all the Greek stuff you downloaded the night before. So, spill. What's really going on?"

Paige brushed her hand through her hair. "Okay, to tell you the truth, he scares me a little."

Phoebe leaned forward. "Why?"

"Because he could be . . . perfect. He could really be the one."

"Whoa. Paige, this is—"

"Yes. This is big. It's also why you haven't met him. Why I can't seem to . . . I don't know . . . function normally?"

Phoebe moved closer. "Paige, honey, this is exactly when you need us. Let us meet him. We'll do the Power of Three guy radar thing."

"I'd like that. In fact, I was hoping you both could come to the museum."

"Is that really the best way to meet him? In

the middle of tours full of . . . ancient boredom?"

"Maybe not," Paige admitted, "but that's not the only reason why I'd like you to stop by."

"Oh? Some other hottie's in the running and you want us to help you decide?"

"No." Paige gave her sister a look that said, *Very funny.* "No, there's this—thing—that's part of the exhibit, and it doesn't seem like it's just an artifact." She changed the computer screen to the museum's Web site, pulling up a shot of a section of the Greek exhibit.

The image showed several of the antique pieces, each on its own display stand. "This isn't a very good picture, but take a look at this item here." Paige pointed at a football-size white object. "It's supposed to be an ancient stone carving of a mythical dragon's egg, but I get the feeling that it's a lot more than that."

Phoebe leaned over, studying the object. She passed her hand over the computer screen slowly, carefully. "I can't get a reading off of a computer image," she said, "but it does seem creepy."

Paige nodded, her suspicions strengthened. "Can you and Piper come down? Check it out?"

"Sure. When do you go back to the museum?"

"I'm there this afternoon until five."

"I'll be finished before then. I'll pick up Piper and we'll stop by."

"Thanks, Sis."

"Now, shoo." Phoebe waved Paige out of her

chair. "Let me get back to my actual job. You know, the one where *other* people ask for my advice."

Paige left, both relieved and troubled that Phoebe had seemed to confirm her suspicions about the dragon's egg.

Later that afternoon, Phoebe walked out of her building while calling Piper on her cell. She filled Piper in on the plan. "So just tell me where to pick you up," she said. "We still have time to get to the museum before the last tour."

"I'm at P3."

"Is Wyatt with you?"

"No. I left him with Leo today."

"Piper? You sound so down. What's wrong?"

Piper breathed out a long, slow sigh into the phone. "I'll tell you all about it when you get here."

Phoebe picked Piper up in front of P3. "Okay," Phoebe said as Piper climbed into the passenger seat, "tell me what's up with you. Because this afternoon is supposed to be all about Paige's guy, and Could He Be The One, and this weird stone egg thing. So you need to clear your head before we get to Lincoln Park."

Piper stared at the traffic in front of them. "I solved the problem with the books."

"Whoa! That's great!"

Piper continued to stare at traffic. "I guess."

"Out with it. What's up?"

"We got this new bookkeeping software. Months ago. It's cool, and labor saving, and kind of like our own special version of a spreadsheet. So I started filling out our orders with it."

"Cut to the good part," said Phoebe. "The drive isn't that long."

"It repeats the order you make from week to week so you don't have to fill it out all over each time."

Phoebe began to guess at what Piper was trying to say. "There's been some mistake repeating itself on the automatic tequila order?"

Piper gave her a tight-lipped smile. "Yep."

"So that's great. You found the problem. Just fix the order."

Piper nodded. "That's the easy part."

"What other part is there?"

"After I reset the books, I went back to balance and found out that now there's *too much* money in the receipts." She rubbed her forehead softly, almost as if she were hiding behind her hand. "You remember that little fear-of-God speech I gave all the employees? It turns out that one of our bartenders, Bernie, really took it to heart. The mistake on the order made it look like the tequila was missing from his till every time. He was so afraid that he might lose his job . . ."

Phoebe caught on. "Bernie started putting his own money in the till to make up for it?"

"Yeah." Piper sat quietly for a moment. "It was my mistake, but I blamed my employees.

Apparently I'm such an evil hag to work for that it's easier to put a third of your night's salary back in the till rather than face my wrath."

"Oh, hon." Phoebe looked for something to say that didn't sound like an answer from her column. "You have to tell him."

"I did. I told him how sorry I was. Then I suggested that maybe next time, if there's a problem, he come to me rather than try to cover it up."

"And he's okay?"

"He seemed relieved. He told me he was planning to quit because he couldn't afford to keep paying for the missing bottle." Piper looked up. "I gave him his money back. I think we're fine now."

"Good," said Phoebe. "That's . . . good. Now, on to other things."

Piper and Phoebe made it to the museum in time for the last tour, and they took it with Chase while Paige led another one. Afterward, Paige joined her sisters. As she walked closer, Piper and Phoebe gave her two thumbs way up.

Piper complimented her sister. "Great job tutoring him, Paige."

"Yeah," Phoebe agreed. "He seems to know his stuff. And when it gets a little boring, he's so gorgeous to look at, you don't mind."

Paige laughed. "So, we can all agree he's a

hunk." She looked back at her sisters. "What else do you see?"

"Potential," Phoebe said. "Definitely. He could be a keeper."

"Tell us what else *you* see," said Piper. "Because there's clearly something else going on here. Otherwise, you'd just date the guy, like any girl does, until you know if you really want a relationship with him."

"It's this *feeling*," Paige said wistfully. "This new vibe. Really strong, especially when I'm near him. Almost like I can't stop myself from . . . I don't know . . . attacking him and sucking his lips right off his face."

"Okay," said Phoebe, "either you're seriously falling for this guy or you're turning into a vampire."

"Very funny." Paige looked around the museum. "They're starting to clear the herd. Let's put Chase on hold until we get home, and go see the dragon's egg before they throw you guys out too."

Phoebe spoke as they walked. "We saw it on the tour. I got some creepy vibes again, but I couldn't very well get my hands on it with all those tourists around."

"It's going to be hard enough without all the tourists," said Paige, "but I think I might be able to let you make contact."

"That should be enough," Phoebe said.

They moved into the section of the exhibit that housed the egg.

The room was darkened, so that the handful of Greek objects looked more impressive under their individual spotlights. This added to the strange malevolence that seemed to emanate from the egg. The sisters stopped in front of it, Piper and Phoebe reading again the information on the small placard next to the egg.

Because it was nearly the same size and shape as a football, the placard stated, it may have been carried in some ceremony. Smooth, carved from solid alabaster, the egg was covered with symbols from two different periods of Greek history. All of the symbols surrounded a single image carved into the rock. The image was of a long, scaly creature with a snakelike body but the head of what could be a dragon. Mouth open, forked tongue extended, wide nostrils, wolflike fangs, and prominent eye sockets did indeed look more like a representation of a dragon than of a snake.

"I think they got it right when they said that it's an artifact that straddles two worlds," said Paige. "But, while the archaeologists who found it think it's some translation from the Mycenaean Greek into the newer Classical Greek, I'm afraid it might be a translation from the metaphysical to the physical world."

"You mean from the demon world to our world," said Piper.

While Piper and Paige talked, Phoebe stared at the egg, moving closer to its pedestal. She leaned over the velvet rope, reaching her hand out slowly.

As Phoebe stretched closer, Piper watched. "Careful," she said, "it's almost . . . glowing."

Phoebe stretched her fingers closer, closer. . . .

"Please do not touch the exhibit pieces," a voice boomed from behind them.

Phoebe jumped, turning toward the voice, and her fingers grazed the egg, barely making contact. She recoiled, horror etched on her face.

Paige spoke to the guard. "Sorry, Fred," she said. "I was just about to tell her the same thing. She's my sister, and she wanted a closer look."

"Look, but don't touch," said Fred. "Besides, we're closed now. So you had best be on your way to the exit."

"We are. Thanks." Paige waited until Fred had turned and left, then she and Piper quickly helped Phoebe to a nearby bench. The three of them sat, with Phoebe in the middle.

"Are you okay?" Piper asked.

Phoebe gasped, still shuddering. She clenched her hands, calming herself. "It's a good thing I didn't get the chance to pick it up," she said. "That thing is not only evil, it's powerful. In just that split second, I saw . . . eons."

Piper brushed Phoebe's hair, working to soothe her. "Eons of what?"

"It's—," Phoebe stopped. "It's too much for me to process right now. But it's like there's something inside it. Sort of an evil genie in a lamp. And it's been waiting a long, long time to get out again."

Piper looked thoughtful. "Well, then, it's a good thing that it's been trapped since the time of the Greeks. It doesn't sound like something that should get out, ever again."

"Yeah, except that I caught a glimpse of the future. If that thing does get out . . ."

Paige picked up the thought. "It could be out for eons?"

Phoebe nodded. "And they will be eons of misery. For everybody."

Chapter Four

Piper and Paige stood in the attic, thumbing through the Book of Shadows. Phoebe sat nearby, wrapped in a blanket, drinking herbal tea.

Paige glanced over. "You sure you're all right?"

"I'll be fine." Phoebe managed a smile. "I can't remember ever feeling this affected for this long after a premonition, but I'm fine. Really."

Piper turned another page in the Book. "I can't find a single reference in here that sounds anything like this demon."

"Maybe that's because this demon is so ancient," offered Paige. "I mean, they think that egg might be three thousand years old. That's way older than anything the Book deals with."

Piper looked to Phoebe. "If a premonition can do this much damage, we can't allow that dragon demon the chance to get out."

Phoebe sipped her tea and nodded. "This is one demon I really don't want to meet up close and personal."

Piper looked at Paige. "What else do we know about the egg?"

Paige ran through her knowledge of the artifact. "It was unearthed in Sparta, and the writing dates from the period called the Greek Dark Age, when the whole civilization went to hell, so to speak."

"Do you think that this egg could have had anything to do with that?" Phoebe wondered. "Could it be that this demon helped destroy the Greek civilization?"

"And when they finally got him back in his shell," Paige guessed, "the Greek civilization took off again?" She thought. "That's definitely a possibility. The Greeks had their best run after that time."

"What's more important to me than the history lesson," said Piper, "is the fact that they did that—they figured out how to bottle up the demon again."

"Then maybe," Paige said, "the newer Greek writing on the egg is sort of a 'how-to' on keeping the demon at bay."

Phoebe joined the conversation. "It's been translated, hasn't it?"

"Yeah," said Paige, "but the translation doesn't make any sense since half of it is in a kind of Greek that's a thousand years older than the words on the other half."

"Maybe the translation makes no sense because the people who translated it weren't looking for a demon," said Piper. She turned to Paige. "See if you can get us a translation from the museum. Maybe it'll make sense to us."

"Can I help?"

The three sisters turned to see Leo at the door to the attic. Piper crossed to him for a quick hug. "How's Wyatt?"

"Sleeping, now," said Leo. "What is it you three are working on up here?"

Piper filled him in quickly.

"Does it sound like anything you've ever encountered?" she asked.

Leo shook his head. "No."

Phoebe stood, setting down her teacup. "Leo, can you ask the Elders?"

"Yeah. From the sound of things, I should ask them now."

Piper gave him a tight smile. "Now would be good."

Leo nodded, then orbed into brightness and vanished.

Paige went back to the Book of Shadows. "It's so rare for the Book not to even give us a hint."

Piper spoke up. "You've given us plenty of hints, so maybe the Book doesn't have to. But I also think it goes back to what Paige said earlier. We're dealing with a demon older than our first ancestor, older than the history of this Book. And because whatever's in that egg has been dormant

for so many centuries, none of the authors of the
Book have had any reason to know about it."

"Until now," added Phoebe.

"Until now," Piper agreed.

Leo orbed back into the attic.

Piper looked up. "Short conversation?"

"Long enough." Leo looked to the three of
them, choosing his words carefully. "You three
seem to be on the right track."

"That's it?" Piper looked a little miffed. "We
ask for help, and the Elders give us a pat on the
head?"

Leo smiled uncomfortably. "Do you remember how the Elders sort of . . . created . . . the
Greek pantheon of gods?"

"Yeah," said Piper. "The Elders had all these
good intentions, but things didn't exactly turn
out the way they wanted."

"Right," said Leo. "And then trying to put
things back into some kind of order . . ."

"Made things worse?" Piper guessed.

"Right." Leo still had that uncomfortable
smile plastered on his face. "This is kind of like
that."

"What are you saying?" Phoebe asked. "That
they don't want to give us any help because
they're afraid it might make things worse?"

Leo worked to put a better spin on things.
"They don't think you need any help right now.
Their position is to let sleeping demons lie, so to
speak."

Paige nodded thoughtfully. "I guess they know what they're talking about. Maybe our trying too hard to keep the demon bottled up would be the very thing that lets it out."

"Works for me," said Phoebe. "If doing nothing keeps what I saw from happening, then I'm all for it."

"It *has* been in that egg for thousands of years now," Piper said, as if she were trying to convince herself. "So I guess we'll just ignore the fact that this egg has been practically dropped in our laps."

"Maybe that's enough," guessed Paige. "Maybe just knowing that it's there, that this evil thing is ready to pounce on an unsuspecting world again . . ." She trailed off, looking from Piper to Phoebe.

Piper finished the thought. "Maybe that knowledge will put us on our guard to make sure that never happens." She arched an eyebrow at her husband. "Is that the message from the Elders?"

Leo shrugged. "Pretty much." He moved closer to Piper. "Just for now, let's try it their way. If things change . . ."

The four of them exchanged a look. They all knew what they'd have to do if things changed.

Paige walked into the now-closed museum café after the last tour of the day. Chase sat by the window, staring at the ocean. Paige smiled and walked toward him, but before she got halfway across the space, Grace Stephens stepped up to him.

Paige stopped, watching the two of them talk for a minute. It looked innocent enough, but Grace was a professional, and if she and Chase were seeing each other, Grace certainly wouldn't let it show at the museum. The thought left Paige cold.

After Grace walked away, Chase gazed at the ocean for a moment longer, then rose.

Watching him, Paige realized that she'd been holding him at arm's length, and now she wasn't sure why. Because she'd hesitated, Grace may have decided to move in. It felt to Paige as if she were in danger of letting Chase slip though her fingers. She decided to try to stop that from happening.

She walked up to him. "Hey," she said.

He turned, smiling. "Paige."

"Um . . ." She looked at him, suddenly unsure what to say. *So you're seeing Grace?* seemed far too possessive, especially since she'd done so little to lay claim to Chase herself. "I saw you talking to Grace. Is everything all right?"

"You're not going to believe this," he said, his smile growing. "The warfare exhibit has become so popular that several people have bumped into the shields on display, just because the crowds are so big. So Grace just asked me to move everything back a couple of feet."

Paige felt relief flood through her. "You have to stay late?"

"Yeah, but who cares?" He fixed her with those incredible eyes of his. "I get to touch the spears, the shields. I get to *hold* a sword that some Greek soldier carried into battle over two thousand years ago."

"Wow." She was still giddy with relief. "Lucky you."

"Hey, you want to help?"

This, thought Paige, was getting better and better. "Sure. And afterward maybe you could buy me a cup of coffee or something."

"I ought to be buying you dinner for a week," he said. "I'm sure I wouldn't have lasted this long at the job without your help. I'd be back in Kansas about now. Instead, I'm here, doing something that I like, that actually feels like real work. Not something that I'm faking my way through." He smiled. "Grace just came and asked *me* to do this. You know what she said? That I show such a *reverence*—that's her word— such a reverence for the war artifacts on my tour that she knew she could trust me with this." He looked at Paige. "And it's all because of you."

For once, Paige couldn't hold his gaze. She looked down. "That's nice to hear," she said. "But it wasn't all me. I think you had it in you all along to be good at this."

"Maybe," he said. "But I still say you bring out the best in me."

Paige looked up, met his gaze, and smiled.

"So," he went on, "after we get the exhibit rearranged, I'd like to do something to show you my appreciation."

"That stuff you just said was a pretty nice thank-you."

"But not a proper thank-you."

Paige got the idea that he was talking about something closer to a kiss than to a dinner, and a surge ran through her. She decided to test her idea. "What would you consider a proper thank-you?"

"I guess buying you a cup of coffee would be a good start."

"A start? And what would the rest of this thank-you look like?"

He stared at her, melting her with those beautiful eyes of his. She decided that if he reached out to her again, like he had at the coffee shop, she wouldn't retreat. She'd grab him and hold on tight.

"Let's get the exhibit squared away first," he said.

They began to walk through the exhibit spaces toward the war room. Chase looked at her. "So, after we've finished here and after I buy you that cup of coffee, for the next part of my thank-you maybe we could go someplace fancy for dinner."

Several thoughts ran through Paige's mind. She tried not to think of what might follow dinner. Instead, she thought about how little they both made on their museum salaries. "Dinner would be nice," she said. "But it doesn't have to be anything fancy. A sandwich at that coffee shop on the beach would be fine."

Chase cocked his head at her. "Are you kidding me? After all the work you did? All the facts you looked up just to pound into my brain?"

"I didn't have to look up most of them. I already knew Greek history."

"Oh? You sure about that? When I first got all into the Trojan War stuff, you came back the next day with tons of information about how the Greeks fought."

Paige smiled, caught. "Okay, maybe I did do a little extra research."

"Only a little?"

"Maybe more than a little."

"And for that, you need to be properly thanked."

Chase stepped into the armor exhibit. "Okay, see the taped-off sections behind these pieces? Grace said we're supposed to move the armor and the stands back that far."

Paige looked at the artifacts, then at the taped squares marked off on the floor behind them. Only a few of the pieces, she noted, needed to be moved in order to give the exhibit considerably more space. Grace had thought this out well. "Looks easy enough," she said. "Let's get started."

Chase picked up a box of disposable gloves. "Here," he said, handing a pair to Paige. "We're supposed to wear these before we touch any artifacts."

Paige took the gloves, smiling as her fingers brushed against Chase's.

Chase donned his own gloves, then turned to the first exhibit piece, a Grecian shield. "I'll hold the shield while you move the stand."

"Sounds good." She watched as he carefully lifted the shield out of its base. The base itself was light, and easy to move. She slid it back until it covered the tape marks. "Okay," she said. "Ready."

Chase placed the shield on his left arm, the way a Grecian soldier would have. He traced the leading edge with the fingers of his right hand. "This is so cool," he said, speaking almost reverently. "I mean, after I learned about how they used their shields"—he lifted the shield on his arm slightly—"how rows of warriors fought side to side, shield to shield"—he picked up one of the spears—"using these first—"

"Chase." Her tone was a gentle reprimand. "We're here to move the pieces, not play Greek soldier."

Chase laughed softly. "I'm waiting for you to move the spear stand."

She smiled, shook her head, and moved the base for the spear into place. "There."

Chase continued to hold the shield and spear, lost in his own world.

"Chase? The stands are ready now."

"Yes, ma'am," he teased. He set first the spear, then the shield, carefully into their support stands.

Chase moved to the swords. "Ready?" She nodded. He lifted one of the swords, holding it carefully while she slid the support base back to its new marks. As she did so, he raised the sword, turning it in his hand, watching the light glint off the blade. "I know now, thanks to you, that these swords were the second line of defense, that the soldiers in the Greek armies only went to their swords when the shield line broke down. That's when they brought out these, and the hand-to-hand combat really started."

"The stand is ready." This time she tried not to sound like she was reprimanding him. She wasn't sure she liked being called "ma'am."

"You've got to hold this," he said, turning to her. "The weight, the heft. Those old sword-making guys really knew what they were doing."

She reached out for it. "I'll put this one back, you get the next one."

Chase smiled as she took the sword. "Can't you feel it? Some Greek soldier really used this very blade centuries and centuries ago." He watched her face, nodding. "You *do* feel it. I can see it in your eyes."

He was right. The sword carried more than its

weight, its heft. It carried its history. And since Chase could feel it too, that meant this was something from the ordinary world, not the charmed world. Or, she thought, it meant that Chase was even more perceptive than she'd first imagined. "Yes," she said. "I feel it. Very cool." She carefully reset the sword into its display case. "Okay. Last one." She waited for Chase to lift out the last sword, then she slid the base onto its new marks.

"I never would have experienced any of this if not for you," he said, holding the sword carefully. "I never would have guessed that something this old could turn me on so much."

She smiled, holding out her hands, taking the sword from him.

Her first instincts about him had been right, she decided. The Chase who felt the power of the ocean was also the Chase who felt the power of antiquity in these weapons. That other part of him, the cheating-on-the-job-application part, that wasn't as important. Yes, tonight would be the time to tell him she wanted to get closer.

While she mused about all of this, staring at the sword in her hands, Chase crossed to the neighboring display, where the egg sat, glowing. "Are we moving this, too?"

She looked behind the egg's stand and saw the tape marks. She had a bad feeling about this. "Um, wait . . ."

"Don't worry. This thing doesn't do it for me

the way the swords and shields do. We can move this and be out of here in two minutes." He reached for the egg.

"Chase, let me move that one."

He looked at her. "How can you? You've still got that sword in your hands. Put that down and let's get this done." In one smooth motion, he lifted the egg.

"Chase, don't." She stepped closer, intending to stop him.

He gave her a curious look. "I'm okay. Just put the sword back and come move the stand for me." He looked back at the egg, holding it in one hand while his fingers traced the symbols etched onto its side. "Hey, this looks like it says '*Eklutos . . . prolegô . . . anoixis . . . ôioskuphion . . . agnôstos*'—'Use extreme caution when opening this egg-shaped object.'" He shook his head. "Wow, I don't know how I knew that."

"Chase, put it back on the stand now!" She reached for the egg with her left hand, still holding the sword in her right.

Too late. The glow coming from the egg brightened, the words burning on the surface. Chase's face went white, but he kept reciting the inscription. "'*Exôthen, alexô achrêstos artitokos ethnos.*'"

Paige frantically searched her knowledge of Greek. "'Finally, I have received a newborn host'?" She tried to pull the egg from him. "Stop! Stop talking now!"

The egg seemed welded to his hands. He looked at her, frightened. "I don't know that much Greek. I don't know what I'm saying."

"Then stop saying anything!"

"I can't!"

His voice continued the incantation, a stream of Greek too complex for Paige to follow, as the words on the side of the egg glowed white-hot.

She heard a distinctive cracking sound. The egg split, a ragged seam shearing it down its middle. A blinding light shot out. Paige winced, raising the sword to shield her eyes. Chase was completely infused in the bright light. A wisp of smoke, or steam, rose from the halves of the egg. It curled near the ceiling, for a moment taking the shape of the dragon etched on the alabaster, then it descended into Chase. The blinding light vanished, and Chase fell to the floor, unconscious, half of the egg in each hand.

As Paige moved forward the wisp rose, this time directly from Chase, taking solid form, becoming Chase's double.

The demon looked down, flexing his arms, and spoke a short phrase in Greek: "*Dokimos meropêïos phroura.*"

Paige, thunderstruck, translated out loud. "'Acceptable human body'?"

The demon looked at her for the first time, regarding her. He repeated the Greek, then mimicked her English: "'Acceptable body.'"

Without warning, the demon lunged at her,

lifting his fists as if to strike. Paige barely had time to raise the sword before the demon impaled himself on it. He staggered back. Paige pulled the sword free, ready to strike again, but the demon sank to his knees, mortally wounded. He clutched his belly, then looked up, whispering, as he collapsed, *"Locheios."*

Paige stood unmoving, confused, translating again. "'Thank you'?"

The demon nodded, managing a feeble smile. He closed his eyes. "Thank . . . you . . ."

He stilled.

Paige rushed to Chase, dropped the sword, and knelt next to him. "Chase? Can you hear me?" She felt for a pulse. Relief swept over her. He was still alive.

Behind her the demon stirred, and Paige heard the sound of flesh being rendered. She turned and watched, horrified, as the demon split in two from groin to neck, joints twisting and popping, bones snapping, flesh tearing. The head was the last to split, as if sliced cleanly down the middle. Then each half quickly grew a second half so that the demon became two.

As soon as Paige realized what was happening, she rose, picked up the sword, and crossed to the demon. She stopped at one of the halves, which was still forming its new limbs, and plunged the sword into its midsection. She put her foot on its stomach and pulled the sword free, but this time there was no damage. The sword came out cleanly, as if she'd pulled it from clay rather than flesh: clay that simply closed over itself and was whole again.

Behind her the second demon rose, a deep chuckle forming in its throat. "Thank . . . you . . . ," it growled. It moved toward her, reaching for the sword.

Almost by instinct, Paige held the sword with both hands and swung it with all her might, bringing it up and across the demon, slicing its neck, severing its head. The headless demon sank to the floor.

Paige retreated next to Chase, breathing heavily. The uninjured demon rose and stood watching while the headless one began the process of splitting in two once more. In only a moment there were three demons. All three turned and began to advance on her as she sat next to Chase.

Paige understood what this meant. Rather than trying to kill the demons again, she dropped the sword, grabbed the halves of the egg, and reached for Chase. She orbed them both out of there.

Chapter Five

Paige appeared in the Manor's living room with Chase, dropping the egg halves as she materialized, struggling to keep Chase from falling to the floor as well. "Piper! Phoebe! Help!"

Piper ran in from the kitchen. "Oh, my—what happened?"

"Chase picked up the egg," said Paige, "and somehow, he let the demon out."

Phoebe, too, rushed in. "He did what?"

The three of them laid Chase on the couch, covering him with a blanket as they spoke.

"I don't know how—okay, I think I do know. But we don't have time for that right now." Paige looked to Phoebe. "Can you stay with him? Make sure he's all right?" She nodded to Piper. "You and I need to get back to the museum. We've got to stop this thing before it goes any further."

"Wait," said Phoebe. "Before you go . . . what are we dealing with?"

"A demon who can double himself," Paige said. "Kill this demon, and it splits in two. And then the way you killed it the first time won't work again."

"Oh, great," said Piper. "This sounds like fun."

"We've got to get back there, before it—they—whatever, hurts the guards at the museum. Before it gets away. I mean, if it's out on the street running amok and the police try shooting it or something, we'll have more demons than we know what to do with." She took Piper's hand, and they disappeared in a flash of light.

Piper and Paige orbed back into the museum just as several guards were rushing down the hall toward the war artifacts display. With a wave of her hand, Piper froze them in place. She turned, concentrating, closing her eyes, and waved her hand again, this time slower, in a larger arc. She looked at Paige. "That should freeze anyone still in the museum." She looked around. "Where's the demon?"

"You mean the three demons."

"Right."

Paige turned in a circle, trying to sense the evil coming from the demons. "Not here," she said. "Not all that close, anyway."

"Okay." Piper thought a moment, looking over the clear signs of a struggle around her.

"Let's do damage control, then go try to find him." She corrected herself. "Try to find *them*."

"I'll straighten this up," said Paige. "I know how the exhibit should look." She stared up at the security camera high in the corner of the ceiling. "Can you pull the surveillance tapes? They'll all be in the—"

"The security office. Sure." Piper looked to the three frozen guards, who each wore a look of concern on his face. "But even if we take those security tapes, this is going to be hard to cover up."

"One thing at a time," said Paige. She picked up the box of gloves. "Here," she said. "Wear these. The last thing we need to do is leave our fingerprints all over the place."

Piper nodded her agreement. She took a pair of gloves and left for the security office while Paige carefully reset the exhibit stands.

A few minutes later, Paige entered the security office. She glanced at the guard on duty. The guard's body was frozen, leaning in at an angle, on her face a look of concentration. Her eyes were set on the screen, which showed the egg display and the three unmoving guards. Paige looked at Piper. "Everyone in the museum—not that there are all that many people here now— but every one of them is still frozen. You're really good at that."

"Practice," said Piper, "may not have made me perfect, but it's made me a lot better." She turned to the bank of tape recorders. "As near as I can figure, the egg display would have been visible from three of the security cameras." She held up three tapes. "I pulled these."

"Then let's get out of here. The sooner you unfreeze everyone, the better."

"The sooner we find that demon—demons— the better." She looked at Paige. "What about the egg? They're surely going to notice that it's missing."

"True," said Paige. "But we might need it if we're going to learn how to destroy that demon."

"Good point." Piper held out the tapes. "Why don't you take these back to the Manor for safe-keeping? I'll meet you out in front of the museum."

Paige nodded and disappeared in a stream of light. Piper headed for the entrance.

As she left the museum and stepped out into the park, Piper gestured, unfreezing those inside. She guessed that the three guards, suddenly walking briskly again, would notice that things were different from the way they'd been before, but she had no time to worry about that right now. She turned, looking for a path the demons might have taken.

Paige appeared in the living room. She set the tapes down and quickly crossed to where Phoebe sat beside Chase. "How is he?"

Phoebe looked up. "Good news? He's awake." She looked back to Chase. "Bad news, he's paralyzed. Can't move anything except his eyes. So he's been blinking at me." She glanced at her sister. "I'm pretty sure he understands what I'm saying, but I doubt that he has any idea what's going on."

Paige knelt next to Chase. "If you can understand me, blink twice."

Chase blinked once, then again.

"Good." She reached up, stroking his hand. "Can you feel that?"

He blinked twice again.

She nodded, smiling. "Good." She stroked his hand again softly. "Do you remember what happened?"

For a moment Chase didn't respond, his eyes searching back and forth, as if trying to find a memory. He blinked once.

Paige nodded. "It's all right. We're going to take good care of you. Don't worry about a thing." She rose and stepped away from the couch, motioning for Phoebe to follow her. They crossed into the kitchen.

Paige spoke softly. "Do you think he saw me orb in?"

"Hard to tell what he can see. Or hear." Phoebe, too, spoke quietly.

Paige glanced back toward the living room. "I've got to get back. Piper's looking for the demon."

"So he's gone?"

"Yeah."

Phoebe shuddered. "Something tells me you won't have much trouble finding him again. Just follow the trail of destruction."

"I'm hoping we can find him—them—before it gets to that."

"Good luck," said Phoebe, but she didn't look hopeful.

"I remember what you saw," said Paige. "We'll try our best to get the demon corralled soon." She indicated the living room. "Can you stay here with Chase?"

"Sure. I'll surf the Net while you're gone, look for info on the egg."

"Good idea." Paige glanced once more at the living room. "I really want to stay with him, but I need to get back before—"

"Don't worry, I'm here," said Phoebe. "You should hurry."

Paige orbed away and was gone.

She appeared next to Piper in the park. "Anything?"

Piper shook her head. "It's quiet, almost deserted. Which is strange, for such a beautiful day."

Paige looked around. It was indeed beautiful. The sun was lower now, but still wouldn't set for another two hours. It was far warmer than the last time Paige had been at Land's End, the day she'd first seen Chase, over three weeks ago now.

"So, I guess it's true," she mused out loud. "I really was meant to meet Chase. Except that I can't believe I was meant to teach him enough about Greek history to cause him to set a terrifying triple demon loose."

Piper laid a reassuring hand on her sister's shoulder. "Just another little irony in our lives, I guess."

Paige looked at her watch. "It's almost six, so it's still rush hour. We've got a demon—three demons, really—that speak no English except 'acceptable body' and 'thank you.'" She stopped, seeing Piper's confused face. "I'll explain later. Right now, let's try to figure out why there's no one in the park."

Piper heard the *thup-thup-thup* of rotor blades and looked up to see a news helicopter circling over the far end of the park. "I have a feeling our answers—and our demons—are that way."

Paige nodded. The two of them took off running across the park.

They arrived to see the remnants of an auto accident, one bad enough to snarl traffic into the park. Both looked around quickly, scanning the paramedics, the police redirecting traffic, the news camera crew.

Piper frowned. "This is all so . . ."

"Normal."

Piper nodded. "Our demons aren't here."

"So what do we do?" Paige looked around, frustrated. "Go home and watch the news and wait until three identical triplets lay siege to the city?"

Piper watched the crowd. "I think that's exactly what we do."

At the Manor, Paige checked in on Chase, who was asleep. She covered him gently, then moved to Phoebe, who was sitting at her computer and printing out pages about the egg. "What did you find?" Paige asked.

Phoebe indicated the pages that were still printing out. "This is all the stuff from the museum here, plus a few pages from the lending museum in Athens." She looked up at Paige. "Sorry for the bad pun, but it's all Greek to me. I was hoping you could tell us what it means."

Paige picked up the pages, which had finished printing, and began to read them. "Good work," she said. "This explanation from Greece is far more extensive than the one we got at the museum." She read further, then turned and walked to where Piper sat studying the halves of the egg. "At least they don't seem to be glowing anymore," Paige observed.

"Whatever energy they housed," said Piper, "is now in that demon."

Paige picked up the egg halves, rolling them in her hands, holding them under a lamp. She fitted the two halves together, reading the inscription again. "That's funny," she said.

"What?"

Phoebe joined them as Paige translated the first inscription out loud: "'This is the egg of the dragon.'" She turned the egg over, reading the other side. "'The dragon must never be hatched.'" She went back to the pages Phoebe had given her, paraphrasing them for Piper and Phoebe. "There are several things that have always been puzzling about this inscription, and how it should be translated."

"Tell us," Piper said.

"The first, and most obvious, is the language." She ran her finger over the words *This is the egg of the dragon*. "These words are a thousand years older than the second half." Here, she traced the words on the other side of the egg: *The dragon must never be hatched*.

"Right," agreed Piper. "A thousand years older. Bad dragon. We know that."

"That's always puzzled archaeologists. They couldn't figure why someone went back to an old, old, rock and wrote on it again."

Piper was ahead of her. "But *we* know that the second part was a warning."

"Yes," Paige said. She read further into the pages. "Archaeologists have also been puzzled by the repetition of the word 'dragon.' Some have always thought it could mean dragon, plural."

"It could mean two dragons?" Phoebe guessed.

"Maybe more than two." Paige traced the words again. "And the word 'hatched' has always given them problems too. Some think it should be translated as 'released.'"

"Maybe that makes less sense to them, but it's making more sense to me," said Piper.

Phoebe leaned in, but Piper held up a hand. "Let's keep you away from this, for now."

"Got it," said Phoebe. "You two do the close-up work."

"Now, back to the word 'dragon.'" Paige pointed to one half of the egg, then the other. "See? This word, right here, is 'dragon' in the older Greek." She traced the Greek with her fingers, pausing on a word. The crack ran right through the middle of it. She turned the egg over to the other side. "And this word translates into 'dragon' in the newer Greek."

Piper studied the egg. "The crack runs right down the middle of that word on each side."

"Yes," said Paige. "And when I pull the egg apart"—she moved her hands slightly away from each other, separating the egg again— "now each half of the word 'dragon' makes two new words."

Piper leaned closer, looking at the egg. "What are the new words?"

Paige moved to her Greek reference books. "Should be able to find it in one of these," she said.

As Paige looked through first one translation

book, then another, Phoebe watched. "Amazing. You bought a whole library just to impress a guy."

"Shhh," said Piper. "He's paralyzed, he's not deaf. And he's right over there."

"Sorry."

Paige turned back to them. "Well," she said, "this makes things more interesting."

Piper looked up. "What do those two new words translate into?"

"'Ravaging Hydra.'"

Piper rephrased this. "Hydra on a rampage?" She frowned. "Isn't Hydra the monster that grew two heads every time you chopped off one?"

"Yes," said Paige, moving back to the egg. "And look at this." She pointed to the scales on the etching of the dragon. "Look closely. See how each scale looks like a tiny dragon's head, and each head is uncurling?"

Piper peered at the rock. "They do." She looked over the dragon etching. "There must be hundreds of them." She thought for a moment. "Someone took a very long time to carve these tiny, tiny details. They were definitely trying to tell us something."

"How," Paige asked, "are we going to explain hundreds of Chases running amok in the city?"

Phoebe looked at her watch. "Speaking of that, the news is on."

Piper walked over and turned on the TV just

in time to hear the announcer say that there would be a story about the theft at the museum, right after the next commercial.

Paige crossed the room and sat next to Piper. Phoebe joined them. In all the concern over the demon, Paige hadn't thought of this.

The newscaster came back after the break, and the three sisters watched, all of them leaning forward unconsciously as the story unfolded.

The newscaster nodded to the camera. "Today's top local story: A priceless Grecian artifact was stolen from the Legion of Honor Museum in a daring daylight drama that developed just after the museum closed."

"Who is this news guy," asked Phoebe, "Mr. Alliteration?"

Over pictures of the missing egg and other shots of the exhibit, the newscaster droned on. "Police now expect the theft to be the work of this man"—a shot of the egg was replaced by a photo of Chase—"an employee of the museum who was seen leaving the exhibit just after the theft occurred." The photo of Chase was replaced by security tape of the demon, looking like Chase, walking out of the room that housed the egg.

"I should have thought of that," Piper said. "We pulled the tapes of the demon emerging from the egg, but not the hallway tapes of the demon walking out of the room."

Paige grew concerned. "So there's *one* of him. Where are the other two?"

The doorbell rang. The Charmed Ones jumped up. Piper turned off the TV as Phoebe peeked out of the window. "It looks like the police," she said.

Piper ran to the couch where Chase lay. "Leo?" In a moment, Leo appeared beside her. "Can you take Chase up to the attic? Right now?"

"Got it." Leo touched Chase and orbed him away.

Seconds later, Piper heard Leo call out. She ran up to the attic. Behind her, the doorbell rang again.

Piper entered the attic to see Leo leaning over Chase, who was gasping for breath. Panic flooded Chase's eyes.

"Something's wrong," said Leo. "As soon as we left the living room, he started having trouble breathing."

Paige ran into the attic, the halves of the egg in her hands. "Phoebe's answering the door. I thought we'd better hide these before we—" She saw Chase and stopped. "What's wrong with him?" She crossed quickly to his side, still holding the egg halves.

As soon as she got close, Chase's face relaxed, and his breathing returned to normal.

Paige looked down at the halves of the egg in her hands. She looked back at Piper.

Piper read the look on her face. "He can't be out of the presence of the egg and survive."

Paige put the halves of the egg down next to the cot where Chase lay. "So how do we—"

"Oh, Paige?" Phoebe's voice floated up the stairs.

Paige gave Piper a small smile. "Guess we know who the police want to talk to." She left the attic and headed down the stairs. Piper followed her.

Phoebe stood at the door talking to two plainclothes detectives as Paige walked up, Piper following behind her.

"I'm Paige. Can I help you?"

The first detective pulled out a photo of Chase. "We understand you work at the museum, and we'd like to ask you some questions concerning this man and today's theft."

Paige nodded. "Okay."

"We have reason to believe that he had help in this theft."

"What leads you to think that?" Paige immediately wondered if the question made her look guilty.

"Some surveillance tapes are missing. According to the time stamp on the tape of the suspect leaving the museum, the security tapes were taken after he walked out of the museum's front doors."

Piper glanced at Paige. "Really?"

"We understand from Grace Stephens that you and this man were friends?"

"Yes." Paige tried not to look too guilty. "We

were hired at the same time, and we did some research together." Thinking that that made things sound even worse, she quickly added, "For the exhibit. So we could, you know, give better tours." She smiled.

"You were seen talking to him just after the museum closed today."

"Yes. We were rearranging an exhibit, then we were going to head out for coffee."

"What changed your mind?"

"I'm sorry?" Paige felt certain that she would give herself away with the next words she uttered.

"You say you were going out for coffee, but the tapes show him leaving the museum alone. And they don't show you leaving at all."

"No. I had to cancel." *This is it*, she thought. *This is where he pulls out his handcuffs and arrests me.*

Another car pulled up, and a familiar face got out, joining the detectives on the porch.

The detective questioning Paige turned to the newcomer. "Lieutenant Morris."

Darryl smiled. "What have you got, Mike?"

The detective quickly recounted his conversation with Paige up to that point.

Darryl nodded. "Would you mind if I took over from here? The mayor is really breathing down our necks on this one and wants it to be a top priority."

"No problem," Mike told him. "We're due to check out the museum, anyway."

Darryl gave him a tight smile and watched as the two detectives walked back to their car.

"Your timing," said Piper, "is impeccable."

"Glad I could help. Can I come in?"

In the living room, the Charmed Ones filled Darryl in. He frowned when they told him about the ancient demon now released.

"That's your department," said Darryl. "Mine is to solve a theft at the museum." He turned to Paige. "And to determine who was involved."

Paige looked at him helplessly. "How do I help you solve the theft without admitting that I was involved?"

"Let's keep it simple," said Darryl. "Can you tell me that you didn't take the egg?"

Paige gave him a funny, pleading look.

"Oh." Darryl seemed thrown.

"That egg," said Piper, "is the resting place of a powerful demon. Now—without admitting that we have any information regarding its where-abouts—can you appreciate that whoever wants to destroy the demon might need the egg?"

Darryl scratched his head. "Okay . . . can you tell me that you don't know where Chase is?"

Paige gave him the same pleading look.

Darryl buried his head in his hands, sighing deeply. "Let's try something else." He looked up again. "How about if I tell you what I know."

"Sure," said Phoebe. "Whatcha got?"

"At approximately five thirty this afternoon, someone stole a priceless Greek artifact from the museum." He looked at Paige. "We know you work there. We know Chase works there. We know both of you were in the proximity of the stolen artifact at that time." He paused. "We also know that someone took three security tapes *simultaneous* to the time of the crime. We're dusting the security room for fingerprints now."

"Okay," said Piper.

Darryl stared at her, weary. "Should I be concerned about those fingerprints?"

"No. Not at all." Piper nodded to him. "Tell us what else you know."

Darryl thought for a moment, watching the sisters. "There are a few details we aren't releasing to the press . . . because they make no sense."

"Maybe we can help with that," said Phoebe. "What details?"

"For one, Chase wasn't seen leaving the museum just once. He left three times. From three different exits. But nowhere on the tapes is he seen reentering the museum before leaving again."

"That's because . . . ," Piper looked to Paige and Phoebe, who indicated that she should continue. "That's because this demon can replicate himself."

Darryl tried to understand. "So there are three of them?"

"Yeah. Maybe more by now." Piper hesitated, then went on. "Every time you kill this demon, he splits in two."

"I tried—" Paige stopped herself. "We have reason to believe that someone tried to kill this demon, twice, before he left the museum."

Darryl sat, his face a blank mask. "I'm not going to respond to that just yet." He moved on. "Let me tell you what else we don't want the press to know."

"Sure." Phoebe tried to sound helpful.

"One of the museum guards was late coming in to the security office on the shift change. When she got there, she swears she saw signs of a struggle. Exhibit pieces knocked over . . . a sword on the floor . . ." He paused. "But when the three floor guards she alerted got there, everything was back to normal, except that the egg was gone."

Piper raised an eyebrow. "Anything else?"

"Yeah. One more curious detail. There are three security tapes missing, but there was never a time when at least one guard wasn't in that room. So the guard who was late, and whose story makes no sense, is downtown right now, answering questions at precinct headquarters."

"Poor Gloria," said Paige.

Darryl threw her a look. "How do you know it was Gloria?" He looked at Piper. "Do I even want to ask that question?"

"I think," said Piper, "that you might want to take Gloria's statement and send her home. Her being late for her shift as the theft was occurring is probably just a coincidence."

"Actually," Paige added, "it's a coincidence that's best for everybody, especially for her."

"She's an Innocent, then?" Darryl asked. Piper nodded. He stood. "Okay. I'll go see if I can get Gloria off the hook." He looked at the sisters. "And if the three of you happen across any new information regarding any of this—"

"We'll be sure and let you know." Piper crossed to Darryl and hugged him. "It's always good to see you," she said, "and I'm really glad that you conduct such patient, thorough investigations."

"Hey," he said, "you three have been a big help to me. I'm glad to return the favor. But please make sure I don't have to be too patient, or people will start asking questions."

"We want this over quickly too," Piper told him. "We think this demon excels at destruction. On a really big scale."

"So what else is new?" Phoebe asked dryly.

"Let me know how else I can help," said Darryl.

"We will." Piper walked him to the door.

Darryl stepped out onto the porch, then turned, looking as if he wanted to say something more. "Good night," he managed.

"Night." Piper closed the door behind him.

As Piper thumbed through the Book of Shadows, Phoebe checked on Chase. "Still sleeping," she said softly as she walked back to Piper and the Book. "What are you looking for?"

"A spell," said Piper. "Or a potion that we can use against that demon." She stopped flipping pages and looked up at Phoebe. "What did Paige say . . . "

"Is that a question for me, or are you talking to yourself?"

"When Paige was looking at the egg, she told us that the crack had split the word 'dragon' into two new words." Piper thought for a moment. "'Ravaging Hydra.' That was it." She looked through the Book once again, searching. "I know I saw something like that in here somewhere." She stopped. "This is it. 'The Ravaging Man-Beast.'" She read from the Book:

> Do not leave this beast for dead,
> Or two will rise up in its stead.
> Then four more will follow you,
> And eight, sixteen, and thirty-two.
> Until you face a man-beast legion
> Laying waste unto your region.

"That doesn't really tell us anything new," said Phoebe. "What are we supposed to do if we can't kill it?"

Piper flipped through the Book again. "I'm sure there's something in here. . . ."

"Keep looking," said Phoebe. "I'm going to check and see if Paige has seen any stories on the news about our demon. After all, we know he's not going to stay quiet for long."

Phoebe turned and headed out of the attic. Piper continued turning pages, hoping that, somewhere within the Book, the answer to how to stop this demon would reveal itself. She tried not to think about what might happen if she was wrong about that.

Chapter Six

After dinner, Paige and Piper finished cleaning up just as Phoebe came into the kitchen. "It's started," she said.

The sisters moved to the living room, where a late-breaking news bulletin played out. "A convenience store was robbed," Phoebe explained. "The guy on the surveillance footage looked just like Chase. The store owner put three slugs into him, and he staggered out the door and disappeared."

"He's adapted fast to our century," said Paige. "He understands what stores are, and must at least have learned the words 'This is a stickup.'"

"He hasn't been out long, so he couldn't have learned all that much," said Phoebe. "That should be a break for us, right?"

Piper crossed to a chair and pulled out a pen and a piece of paper. "Three demons left the museum," she said as she wrote. "And if the convenience store owner shot one of them several times, we have to assume that demon died and split again. So that makes four."

"Are they all immune to gunfire now," mused Paige, "or just the one who got shot and his new clone?"

"Something tells me we're going to find out soon enough," said Piper. "In the meantime, we've got to keep track of all of them. We'll have to make sure—as soon as we've figured out how to vanquish it, or them—that we get them all."

"Right." Paige rubbed her forehead, worried. "How do we explain to Darryl that his officers can't shoot this guy now?"

"Let me work on that one," said Piper.

"Okay," Phoebe said. "Let's go track them down."

"One thing first," said Piper. "I want to make up a few demon-bashing potions."

"But they won't work," said Paige. "Not on this demon, anyway."

"If it comes to either killing this demon—and letting him duplicate himself again—or letting an Innocent die, I think we have to go for killing him."

Paige sighed. "That only makes our job harder, doesn't it?"

"I don't see that we have a choice." Piper headed up the stairs. "Besides, this is just a backup in case we can't do anything else."

"You should have been a Girl Scout," said Paige, following her. "You know, 'Be prepared.'"

"That's the Boy Scout motto," said Piper, "and I never had any desire to be one of those."

Piper crossed to the Book while Paige checked on Chase.

As Paige approached the cot where Chase lay, she could see him tracking her with his eyes. She smiled. "Hey," she said, "you're awake." She sat beside him carefully. "You must feel like some fugitive that we're hiding in the attic or something."

He watched her, waiting.

"As a matter of fact, you kind of are. The police think you stole that egg from the museum." She watched him for a moment, realizing that he couldn't respond unless she asked him a question. "Are you hungry?"

He blinked once.

"Thirsty?"

He blinked twice.

"Let's start with some water." She rose and left, glancing at Piper as she did so.

Piper looked from Paige to the cot. Chase couldn't see her at the Book from where he lay. "How do I stop a demon that I can't vanquish?" she murmured to herself quietly.

As she paged through the Book, she came upon a possible answer:

> *To stop a demon in his tracks*
> *Although he will not stay,*
> *To hold a demon fast until*
> *You make your getaway,*
> *Use banyan root, and say these words,*
> *'Be still!' And like the tree,*
> *His limbs will root into the ground*
> *And you, dear, will be free.*

"Sounds a lot like freezing to me," Piper mumbled, but she wrote down the directions on how to prepare the banyan root; perhaps her sisters would need such a potion.

She looked for another spell.

Paige returned with a glass of cool water and a straw. She sat beside Chase again. "This might take a bit of trial-and-error research," she said.

His eyes watched her, waiting.

"I'm going to open your mouth, just a little." She reached her hand to his face, her fingers brushing his lips with light, careful strokes. "Can you feel that?"

He blinked twice.

"Good." She pressed on his lower lip, gently opening a small space. She took her hand away. "Hey, it stays open." She smiled at him. "Okay, here goes." She lowered the straw into the glass of water, then covered the end with her forefinger, lifting the straw out of the glass. She placed the straw, now full of water, over his slightly open mouth and lifted her finger. The water, one strawful, poured in.

"Can you feel that?"

He blinked twice.

"Can you swallow?"

He blinked once.

"Okay. Let me try to help." She moved her hand to the point of his chin, softly sliding her fingers down his throat. As she did, he swallowed. "Good," she said. She filled the straw again.

Piper found one more spell to stop a demon: one that would temporarily blind him. She also copied a potion that would banish almost any demon. The last one, she hoped, would send this demon to the netherworld without causing it to split again, but she couldn't be sure. She decided that a bad solution was better than no solution at all. She looked up and for a moment watched Paige, who sat beside Chase as she went through the same steps: dropping in a straw's worth of water, gently stroking his throat, which prompted him to swallow, then doing it over again. By now, the glass was nearly empty.

Piper crossed to her. "I've got those recipes I was looking for," she said, holding up her notes. "I'm going downstairs to make sure we have all these ingredients. I can whip them up quickly."

Paige nodded. After Piper left the attic, Paige looked back at Chase. "I'll bet you've got a lot of questions," she said.

He blinked twice.

"I wish I knew what to tell you. My sisters and I are looking for answers too. For now, you need to concentrate on getting back to normal, and the rest we can deal with later."

His eyes watched her, unblinking.

Paige thought she understood his reluctance to accept this as an answer. "I'm sorry I can't be more helpful." She changed the subject. "Now that we've got this swallowing thing down, we're going to need to feed you too. Broth, I think, to start. Are you sure you're not hungry?"

His clear green eyes watched her, almost seeming to smile.

"Right," she said, embarrassed. "I need to stick with easy-yes or easy-no questions." She took a breath. "Let me try that again. Would you like to have some broth?"

He blinked twice.

"Okay, then," she said, tucking the blanket back under his chin, stroking his shoulder as she did so. "I'll go whip some up. Be back in a bit." For a moment she left her hand on his shoulder, looking to reassure him, wondering what else she could say or do to make him more comfortable. She smiled, softly squeezed the shoulder under her fingers, and rose, walking out of the attic.

As Paige joined Piper and Phoebe in the kitchen, Piper was finishing the third potion while Phoebe bottled the first two. "What did you find?" Paige asked.

Piper pointed. "That one will blind him temporarily, that other one will root him in place for a while, and this one will send him to the netherworld." She looked at Phoebe. "What we really need is a way to track him—them. To find them before the police do, before the news does."

"Let's try that convenience store," said Phoebe. "Maybe I can pick up something there."

"Oh, goodie," Piper said sarcastically, "another place for us to be seen by the police."

"You two go off and have a good time," said Paige. "I'm making something for Chase to eat."

"Wish us luck," said Piper. She and Phoebe left.

The sun had settled lower over the water, but the evening was still bright as Piper and Phoebe got out of the car and walked closer to the convenience store. It was closed, dark. DO NOT CROSS crime tape snaked everywhere, but the police had moved on.

"This could be a break for us," said Piper. "The less we have to explain to our boys and girls in blue, the better."

Phoebe stopped walking, reacting as if she'd been hit by something.

Piper watched her, concerned. "Phoebes? You okay?"

"I see—waves of things. Already. Even at this distance." She took a small step closer, reacting again. "Whoa."

"Tell me what you see."

"So many things. Like several movies playing at once." She winced. "This is circuit overload." She stepped back one foot, then two. "That's better," she said.

"So, what just happened?"

"This is a new one," said Phoebe. "These are some of the most powerful visions I've ever felt. I mean, we're still, what, fifteen feet from the door?" She looked down. "He must have walked here." Gingerly, she stepped closer for a moment, then stepped back again. "I think they're all connected somehow, these different visions. 'Cause I saw—all these movies—running faster and faster, all cramming into my head. . . ."

"That does sound powerful."

"Yeah," said Phoebe. "This one's going to be tough." She looked at her sister. "But I think I have an answer to that whole 'it-them' question. It's one thing, one mind. I have no idea how it can function on so many different levels, but it's got plans for all kinds of destruction, and all of them will be violent."

"Did you see anything that could help us figure out where he's going to strike next?"

"Maybe several things. Let me try to sort them out." Phoebe sat down on the curb. "I saw an explosion, and a building on fire. And one of the demons dying in that fire, then rising as two. At the same time, I saw a suicide pact—some woman and a demon—and they leaped off a

building together. Then," she went on, shuddering, "after they hit, two demons got up again."

"Suicide shouldn't count," said Piper. "That
shouldn't be a way for him to replicate himself."

"I guess it counts if you take somebody with
you."

Piper sat on the curb too. "Can you identify
either of these places?"

Phoebe thought for a moment. "When I saw
the suicide, I saw it from their point of view."

"Where were you?"

"I could see several tall, narrow openings in
the building we were standing in." She closed
her eyes, putting herself back into the vision. "I
can see the city skyline shining at me in long,
narrow strips from beyond these openings. All
the buildings are close, lit up in the night. It's
beautiful. We're walking now, turning a corner,
then another, and I can see the bridge, the water.
It's darker on this side. It's still so . . . beautiful. I
rest my hand on one of the tall columns.
Sandstone, I think. It feels cool under my hand.
We step closer to the edge. I look down. There's
something just under us on the side of the building. It's . . . a giant clock face. We hold hands,
lean forward, and now we're falling past the
clock. The ground is rushing at us—," Phoebe
stopped, visibly retreating from the image.

"It's got to be the clock tower of the old Ferry
Building," Piper said, and put her arm around
Phoebe. "You okay?"

"Yeah. It was just so . . . intense. And it happened so fast. And there were so many other visions, all crammed in like movies in fast motion."

"I know it's a lot to ask . . . did you happen to see what time it was on that clock?"

"It just rushed by." Phoebe closed her eyes. "Ten? Ten . . . forty-five."

Piper looked at her watch. "It's just after eight now. We've got time." She looked at Phoebe. "Now, what about that fire?"

Phoebe thought. "Everything is burning. It's a big fire. Lots of destruction from the explosion." She stopped. "Across the street, in one window that's only half broken, I can see letters. . . ." She traced the letters in the dirt at her feet.

Piper watched her, reversing the order of the letters from the mirrored reflection. "PacBell." She looked to Phoebe. "He's going to blow up the PacBell Building?"

"I think so. And I think it's going to be tonight."

"Which one do we try to stop first?"

Phoebe thought, closing her eyes. "In the fire, it's not quite dark yet."

"So it has to happen first."

"Yeah," said Phoebe. "And there's lots more bodies."

Piper looked grim. "Two reasons to get there first."

Phoebe rose, dusting off the back of her jeans. "Let's go."

Chapter Seven

As Piper drove them up Market Street, Phoebe glimpsed the Transamerica Pyramid peeking out at her from between the other skyscrapers. "He's going to hit that, too," she said, nodding at the building's tall spire as they crossed an intersection. "It was in one of those visions racing by."

"He's going to lay waste to downtown," Piper guessed. "He's here to start another Armageddon."

"Should we call Darryl? Tell him about the PacBell Building?"

"We're going to need all the help we can get," said Piper. She handed her cell phone to Phoebe. "Can you call him? I hate to call while I'm driving. I've already got too much on my mind."

Phoebe punched in his number. "Darryl, it's Phoebe."

"What is it?"

"I saw where he—one of them, at least—is going to strike next."

"Where?"

"The PacBell Building."

"Thanks. I'll get a squad out there right away. Oh, and Phoebe . . . ?"

"Yes?"

"I think it would be better if you and Piper and Paige weren't there, after the—excitement—at the museum."

"We're on our way now," Phoebe admitted. "We'll try to stay out of your way, but stopping the demon is our job. Yours is to save the people if we don't."

Piper could hear the long sigh from the other end of the phone. "Try to stay out of sight when we show up."

"Got it," said Phoebe. "Hope we don't see you there." She hung up, looking at Piper. "Should I call Paige, too?"

"Not unless we have to. Chase is still a vital part of this. He's our link to the demon some-how. When we have a minute, I want to explore that again in the Book of Shadows. So for right now, let's let Paige stay with him." She drove on, quiet for a moment. "If we really need her, she can orb herself to us in a flash."

Paige walked carefully back into the attic, hold-ing a bowl of steaming broth in her hands. She set it down on the table by the cot, then settled in next to Chase. He looked to be sleeping. She brushed his hair lightly with her fingertips. His eyes opened, blinking, focusing on her. "Hey," she said softly. "Were you sleeping?"

He blinked several times.

"I guess it took longer for me to make this than I thought it would." She looked down at him. He was still blinking. She caught on. "You've got sleep in your eyes. We can't have that. It'll mess up our whole code system."

She left, coming back with a bowl of warm water, a washcloth, and a towel. "Close your eyes," she said. She dipped the washcloth into the water and gently washed his eyes, his face, noting the stubble on his chin and his cheeks as she carefully ran the warm washcloth across them. She picked up the towel and patted him dry, then smoothed his hair into place. "Better?"

He blinked twice.

"Good." She put the towel away, then reached for the broth. "This might be too hot," she said. "I'd better taste it first." She filled the spoon and took a sip. "Mmm . . . not too hot, not too cold. I think it would be just right for Goldilocks. Or for you." She filled the spoon again. "I'm not sure how a straw would hold up to hot soup, so let's try this." She moved the spoon to his lips and slowly, a drop at a time, let the broth trickle into his mouth. She put the spoon down and massaged his throat until he swallowed. "Oops," she said, watching an errant drop slide past his lips and onto his cheek. She wiped it with her finger.

The moment was warm, and a little sensual, and reminded her of what she'd wanted to say to him if they'd gone out for that coffee.

"Chase," she said as she readied another spoonful, "I've got a confession to make. Several, actually." She carefully spooned in the broth while she sorted out her thoughts. "I was attracted to you the first time I saw you." She smiled. "And not just because you're such a hunk with your shirt off." She filled the spoon again. "It was because of that thing you said about the power of the ocean." She sat back, forgetting the spoon for the moment. "And then, when I met you at the museum, I kind of held you at arm's length. Maybe because of the jock thing, maybe just because I was scared, I don't know. But today, when I saw you with Grace, I realized what a dolt I'd be if I let you get away. So I was all prepared to tell you how I really feel when . . ." She stopped. "I guess you know the rest." She looked into his eyes. "Anyway, I wanted you to know that. So, when you get better, when we get over all this . . . excitement, I want to go out for that coffee and try again."

His eyes watched hers. After a moment, he blinked twice.

"I just wanted you to know," she said again. She picked up the spoon once more. "This is going to take a while." She smiled down at him. "But don't worry. We've got time."

Piper pulled up to the front of the PacBell Building. "I wonder where we're going to start," she said.

"I wonder where we're going to *park*," said Phoebe. "You can't leave your car on the street."

"Something tells me we shouldn't park near this building," said Piper, "in case we need to get out in a hurry."

Piper parked several blocks away, in a public lot. As they walked back toward New Montgomery Street and the PacBell Building, she tried to formulate a plan. "I guess we want to stake out the place," she said, "and wait for him to show."

She stopped at the corner of Market Street, looking down toward the wharf. She could see the clock tower from there, rising from the end of the financial district only a few blocks away. Even though there were four demons now, they all still seemed to be working close to one another.

The clock on the Ferry Building read 8:20. "The Ferry Building and the PacBell Building are two of the oldest buildings in the city," Piper mused out loud. "Why is the demon starting with old buildings?"

"Maybe because *he's* so old?" Phoebe guessed.

The sisters crossed on the light, walking

toward Mission Street. "Come to think of it,"
continued Phoebe, "how does a demon who
hasn't walked the earth in thousands of years
know about explosives, anyway?"

"Good question."

They crossed Mission and walked the final
block, stopping when they were on the corner of
Minna Street, near the PacBell Building. Piper
stared up at it, then scanned the street. "So," she
said, "I guess we stand around and hope we see
him before he sees us."

"Right." Phoebe looked at the sky. "It
shouldn't be long now. This is what the sky
looked like in my vision."

"Tell me what else you remember," said
Piper. "Any little detail might help."

"It was so . . . jumbled. All those visions cramming in on each other. But I do remember this
building." She cocked her head up at the old
skyscraper, frowning. "It was from the other
side," she said. "I saw the other corner of the
building."

"Then let's walk."

They crossed in front of the building. Phoebe
slowed about a hundred feet on the other side,
craning her head up, peering at the building as
they walked. Piper looked ahead on the sidewalk, keeping an eye out both for a demon
Chase and for any pedestrians Phoebe might
walk into while staring up at the building. Piper
steered her around a woman in a business suit.

"Stop," said Phoebe. She and Piper stood on the sidewalk. "This is what I saw. And a big fire-ball just—erupted. About three or four stories up."

"Good," said Piper. "That's good." She pulled out her phone and hit redial. "Darryl, it's Piper. We're at the building. Phoebe thinks that what-ever is going to happen, it's going to be soon." She watched as Phoebe sank down, sitting on the sidewalk. "Better evacuate the building, just in case," Piper said. "At this hour, that shouldn't interrupt too many people, except the cleaning crews and the workaholics." She hung up and sat down next to Phoebe. "What is it?"

Phoebe rubbed her head. "I've been trying to pull more pieces out of that particular vision," she said, "and it just keeps getting worse."

"Bodies?"

Phoebe nodded. "Probably, like you just said, the cleaning crews, the people working late."

"If he wants to create mayhem," Piper won-dered, "why strike now? Why not strike at noon, or at rush hour?"

Phoebe shook her head. "There is still so much about the demon we don't know."

Piper looked over the block again. "I have this terrible feeling that we may be about to undergo a kind of trial-by-fire-and-error before we find out."

"Let's hope not."

As they talked, several police cruisers pulled up and the officers ran into the building. In only a few moments, people began streaming out.

"Just like we thought," said Phoebe, watching the people stumble out. "Cleaning crews, mostly."

"Yeah . . ." Piper watched the men and women leaving the building, many of them looking confused, scared. One, she noticed, still carried his mop bucket, holding it tightly to his chest. "Except that one looks like Chase."

"Where?"

"The one with the bucket. Let's go." Piper began marching down the sidewalk, heading for the man with the bucket, who wandered slowly on the sidewalk ahead of them, holding the bucket and staring up at the building.

"Piper? What exactly are we going to do when we catch him?"

Piper saw Darryl drive up, his car passing the demon as he pulled to the curb headed the wrong way on the street. Piper moved faster in his direction. "Darryl! Behind you! The man with the bucket!"

As he got out of the car, Darryl turned, locked eyes with the man, and drew his revolver. "Police! Stop where you are!"

The demon kept moving, stumbling as he backed into the street, looking from Darryl to the building.

Phoebe shouted as she caught up with Piper, "He's got a bomb!" She grabbed Piper before she could get any closer and crouched with her behind a squad car. She looked at the potion in Piper's hand, then looked up into her face. "He's got a *bomb*," she repeated. "You can't get close enough to use that."

Two officers on their way into the building turned and headed back to the sidewalk. Darryl stayed behind his car, gun leveled at the demon. "Stop where you are!" Darryl ordered. "Put the bucket down slowly."

One of the policemen who'd just returned to the street, a young rookie, flanked Darryl. He edged closer to the demon, stepping cautiously into the street. "Police!" he said. "Hands on your head."

The demon looked from Darryl to the young officer.

"Back up, Officer Roberts," said Darryl. He spoke to the demon again. "Put the bucket down," he repeated, "now!"

The demon settled his gaze on young Officer Roberts and smiled. Then, with an inhuman roar, he charged the rookie.

Roberts fired three times, hitting the bucket, which the demon still held chest high. The first two bullets passed through the yellow plastic and into the demon with no effect.

The third caused the explosion.

A yellow ball of fire filled the street, lifting Roberts off his feet, throwing him upward and back onto the sidewalk. It blew out the windows of the squad cars and the windows of the lower floors of all the nearby buildings.

Piper and Phoebe hugged each other and pressed against the side of the squad car as the wave of heat and pressure passed over them. They stayed huddled, listening to the sound of glass bursting as it hit the street all around them. When that trailed off, they looked up.

The middle of the street was a blackened scorch mark where the demon had been. Shattered glass littered the sidewalk. Darryl leaned over the rookie, surrounded by piles of glass looking like drifts of sparkling snow. He talked rapidly into his cell phone as he took Roberts's pulse.

He stood when he saw the sisters, moving to them and herding them back from the center of the destruction.

"How is he?" asked Piper.

"He should be okay. His face is burned, and he's lost his eyebrows, but his flack vest saved him from any serious damage."

"Good." Piper scanned the street. "Did you see what happened to the demon?"

"I did." Darryl's voice was grim. "The blast— it blew him apart. I saw it. I looked over to Officer Roberts"—he nodded to the rookie— "and when I looked back, two of them were getting up and staggering off that way." He gestured to the other side of the street.

"Then we failed," said Piper.

"What?" Darryl looked at her sharply. "You

kept that . . . thing . . . from setting off that bomb inside. You saved the lives of everybody on three floors, at least."

"Yeah," said Piper, weary. "But there are five of them now, and we aren't any closer to stopping them."

"You will be. Soon." Darryl placed a comforting hand on her shoulder. "I have faith in you."

Piper smiled. "Thanks. That helps. Really."

The sound of an ambulance approaching caught their attention.

"I should go check for any other injured," said Darryl. "And you two should get out of here, before the press show up. Before any of my officers recognize you."

"Right." Piper sighed, looking at Phoebe. "We know where one of the demons is going to strike next. We'll call you if we need you."

"Do that." He turned to leave, then turned back. "Thanks again."

Piper smiled and nodded. As Darryl walked back toward the destruction, she turned to Phoebe. "What can we learn from this? What was the demon up to?"

"He wanted to get caught," Phoebe said. "He wanted to die."

Piper nodded, getting her sister's drift. "He looked at Darryl, then decided he was better off with the rookie."

"Because he knew, or guessed, that the rookie would shoot."

"But he couldn't die from the gunshot." Piper frowned. "He wanted the explosion to happen."

"So he would be killed by it?"

"I think so. Because every time he's killed, he multiplies."

"And every time he dies," Phoebe reminded her, "he becomes impervious to what just killed him."

"What did the Book say?" Piper thought a moment, then remembered, speaking out loud.

> *Do not leave this beast for dead,*
> *Or two will rise up in its stead.*
> *Then four more will follow you,*
> *And eight, sixteen, and thirty-two . . .*

Phoebe finished the verse for her.

> *Until you face a man-beast legion*
> *Laying waste unto your region.*

"He's building an army," said Piper. "And when it's completed, none of the ways we've stopped him before will work."

"Right." Phoebe looked at her, trying to find an answer in her sister's face. "How do we keep him from doing that?"

"I have no idea."

Chapter Eight

Leo walked into the attic. He saw Paige, slumped forward in her chair as she sat next to Chase. Her head was on his chest as he lay on the cot, her arms on his shoulders, so it almost looked as if they were dancing.

They were both asleep.

Leo crossed to her and shook her shoulder gently to wake her.

She stirred, took a moment to get her bearings, then rose. She covered Chase with a blanket, and she and Leo walked downstairs.

"Have you heard from Phoebe and Piper?"

He shook his head. "They'll call if they need something."

Paige made a face. "I'm not so sure. I mean, they're out there, battling who knows how many of these demons by now. We'll need the Power of Three to defeat them."

"I don't think we're talking about defeat just

yet," said Leo. "I think we're still in the informa-
tion-gathering stage."

"What's really going on with the Elders?"

The question seemed to surprise Leo. He
watched Paige for a moment, thinking. "I don't
know," he said honestly. "Clearly this is some
kind of test for the three of you."

"Or maybe the Elders just don't want to have
to mess . . . *again* . . . with the power of the
Greeks." She looked at Leo closely. "You sure
you don't know any more?"

"I'm sure. If I did, I'd tell you three." He looked
around the Manor. "Wyatt's asleep, Chase is
asleep; maybe one of us should go out and join
Piper and Phoebe."

Paige looked at her watch. "Wow. It's after
ten. I wonder where they are."

Piper looked up at the clock tower, lit in the
dark; the narrow sandstone openings in the
story above the clock glowed as the light shone
out of them. "Is this what you saw?"

"No," said Phoebe. "I saw all of this from
their point of view." She turned and looked at
the brightly lit cityscape of the financial district.
"I saw that," she said, pointing, "but from up
there."

"Okay, then," said Piper. "Let's go."

They entered the structure just as the 10:30
ferry was pulling away. As they climbed their
way toward the floor above the clocks, the last of

the ferry riders and tourists drifted out of the building.

Piper and Phoebe stopped when they heard the quiet voices of a woman and a man coming from the stairwell above them.

"For as long as I've been thinking about this," the woman said, "I've wanted this to be the last thing that I saw."

"Why? It's such a beautiful sight. Why end it all here?"

Phoebe listened to the man's voice. She turned and whispered to Piper, "He sounds just like Chase, only with an accent."

Piper nodded. They crept closer as soundlessly as possible.

"When I first came to San Francisco and rode the ferry, I stepped off and that's what I saw," the woman went on.

"Those lights? Those buildings?" the Chase-like voice asked.

"Yes. And I knew I wanted to work there. Knew I could make a name for myself there."

"And what happened?"

They heard the woman sigh, a long, slow exhale of breath. "Let's just say that to see those lights again is nothing more than a reminder of how far I've fallen short of my dreams."

"So why end it here?"

"In case I need to be reminded of why I'm doing it, why I'm going to jump."

"I see," the man replied.

Phoebe and Piper were close enough now to see the two: a woman, probably in her thirties, dressed in a shabby, thin coat; and the demon, dressed as Chase had been that day at the museum and still looking every bit like him.

The man and woman began to walk around the square, toward the water side of the tower. Phoebe nodded to Piper, and they followed, still moving as silently as possible.

"I'm sorry," said the woman, "I didn't even ask you for your reasons."

"My reasons are my own," said the demon.

"Fine. I'm just glad to have someone with me when I . . ."

Piper and Phoebe stepped closer. Phoebe watched as the woman placed her hand on the sandstone, and she knew that the woman was feeling the coolness under her palm. Phoebe looked to Piper, who fished in her coat for one of her potions.

The woman turned her head at the sound of fabric swishing. "Did you hear something?"

"There may be someone coming," said the demon. He held out his hand to her. "The time is now."

Phoebe turned to see Piper still struggling with the potion. In that moment, the demon looked back, caught sight of them, and, holding the woman's right hand, leaped through the tall, narrow opening in the sandstone.

"Piper!"

Piper gestured, freezing both the man and the woman in place.

Phoebe rushed forward. "Oh, my—" She looked back at Piper. "Hold me! I'm going to try to pull her back in."

"But she's frozen."

"We're not." Phoebe leaned over into space, the ground looming far below her, and reached for the woman's left hand, which was frozen above her head, above the blond hair that now lifted straight up from the woman's scalp. "Hold on to my belt," she said.

Piper got a good grip on Phoebe's belt at the back of her jeans, and Phoebe leaned out even farther.

Phoebe closed her fingers around the woman's wrist. "I've got her," Phoebe said. "Now pull us back in."

Piper tried, but with no success. "Her other hand is still in the demon's."

Phoebe let go of the woman's left hand and leaned over farther, trying to reach the woman's right, which was indeed still tightly in the grasp of the demon's. She stretched her fingers as far as she could. "Can you lower me any farther?"

"Not without dropping you," said Piper. The strain of holding Phoebe was mounting.

Phoebe stretched her fingers once again, reaching until she could barely touch the demon's fingers. She began to pry them from the woman's hand. As she did, she glanced over at the demon's face.

His eyes were watching her.

"Piper! He's unfreezing!"

"He's too powerful for the freeze to hold for long. Hurry! Get his hand off of her!"

Phoebe worked faster, wrenching the demon's frozen fingers away from the woman's one by one.

She pried the woman's thumb away last, freeing the woman completely from the demon. In that instant the demon regained his mobility and grabbed Phoebe's hand. His weight yanked her away from Piper, who watched, helpless, reaching for her sister as Phoebe and the demon fell toward the ground, separating from each other as they did so. Piper couldn't hear Phoebe's screams: Her own were too loud.

Paige appeared next to Piper, peered over the side, and orbed away again. She reappeared next to the falling Phoebe, grabbed her hand, and orbed her away a fraction of a second before they hit.

Piper heard the sickening thud of the demon's body hitting the roof of the marketplace. An instant later, Phoebe and Paige orbed in next to her. Piper put her arms around the shaking Phoebe. "I'll take her," she said to Paige. "Can you get the Innocent? She's still frozen in midair."

Paige orbed away again.

Piper held the quaking Phoebe in her arms, assuring her that she was all right. In a moment they were joined by Paige and the woman.

Piper unfroze the woman, and she collapsed into a heap at their feet. Paige knelt next to her.

The woman looked around, disoriented, mystified. "What . . . what just happened?"

"You were about to make a terrible mistake," said Piper, "but you've been given a second chance."

The woman nodded, seeming to understand. "It *was* a mistake. I'd decided that. Then that man appeared, and he was so . . . mesmerizing."

"The man . . . ," Piper glanced at Phoebe, and they both looked over the side, where two demons stood up, staggered a bit, then began to climb down from the marketplace roof. One looked up at Piper, shouting something.

"Did he just say 'Thank you'?" Piper asked.

Paige, kneeling by the woman, looked up at Piper. "Probably. Long story."

The three sisters turned their attention to the woman, helping her to her feet.

"I don't know how you did that," she said, indicating all three of them, "but I knew what a mistake I'd made the moment I stepped off, and I was so wishing that I could somehow take it back."

"Well, now you can," said Piper. "And the next time things look this bad, remember . . . now you know that nothing is worth throwing your life away for."

"Believe me, I do know that." The woman smiled awkwardly. "I don't know what else to say."

"As long as we know you're safe," said Phoebe, "you've said enough."

The four of them walked down the stairs. At the bottom, the woman looked around, as if for the first time. "I can't believe I almost threw all of this away. I mean, I lost my job, lost my apartment, I'm living out of my car. But still . . ."

Piper took twenty dollars out of her wallet and handed it to the woman.

"No," the woman said. "You just saved my life. That's plenty."

Piper pressed the money gently into the woman's hand. "Now that you have your life back," she said, "go have something to eat—on us—and think about what you want to do next."

The woman hesitated, then accepted the money. "I will," she said. She walked off.

As soon as she was out of sight, Phoebe sat down weakly. "What that woman said about feeling like she just got her life back," she told her sisters, "goes double for me." She shuddered, then looked at Paige. "Thanks."

Piper sat on one side of her, Paige on the other. "I can't remember ever being that scared," said Piper, sliding her arm around Phoebe. "I knew there was nothing I could do in time."

"I guess that's why there's three of us," said

Paige, joining the embrace. "That good ol' Power of Three thing."

Phoebe sighed deeply, as if the hugs were recharging her. "This is nice," she said. "Now, back to business."

"Okay," said Piper. "We did a good job with the Innocents today, but the demon got two more doubles on his side."

"That brings him up to six," said Paige. "Unless he's been busy in ways we don't know about yet."

"Let's go see Darryl," said Phoebe, "and compare notes."

"Good idea," said Paige. "I'll drive."

She orbed the three of them away.

Chapter Nine

"**He's been** busy tonight," said Darryl.

He sat at his desk, looking tired. As he sorted through the pile of printouts in front of him, he motioned to the three sisters. "Please, sit down."

"I hope it's all right, us coming here like this," said Phoebe as the three sat across from Darryl.

Piper told him about the clock tower incident, and the demon splitting again. Darryl nodded wearily. "He's held up two more convenience stores and was shot at one of them."

"What happened?" asked Piper.

"He walked away." Darryl sighed. "The store owner thinks the demon must have been wearing Kevlar, because he hit him in the chest three times. But when we viewed the security tape from his store, it's clear that he's not wearing standard body armor. His shirt isn't bulky enough."

"What do your experts make of that?" asked Paige.

"They're guessing the guy has access to some new, lightweight armor that we don't know about."

"That might work as a cover story," said Piper. "I mean, they know now that it won't do any good to shoot him, right?"

"Our officers have been told that. But that doesn't explain how he can be in several places at once."

"Let me guess," said Phoebe. "You've got crime-scene videotapes of him all over town, taken at the same time."

"Pretty much." Darryl picked up one of the images from his desk. "This one is from eight thirty-two tonight, which is about the time our demon was blowing himself up in front of the PacBell Building." He looked at Piper. "Officer Roberts is going to be fine, by the way, but he's wondering where the body of the perp is."

"What did you tell him?"

"The truth: that we didn't recover one. But as I was saying, at eight thirty-two a man with that same face was robbing a liquor store." Darryl sorted through the papers again. "And at eight thirty-seven, only five minutes later, another camera caught him holding up a gas station about twenty blocks away." He sighed. "How can anyone move that fast?"

Piper looked worried. "These robberies don't fit the pattern we thought we had for this demon," she said.

"What pattern is that?" Darryl asked, putting the papers down.

"He wants to die," Piper told him. "He wants to be killed over and over."

"So he can duplicate himself," Phoebe chimed in. "He wants to build an army."

Darryl nodded solemnly.

"So why is he robbing stores where he's most likely to get shot at again, when shooting him doesn't increase his numbers?" Piper asked.

Darryl looked at her. "Probably for the same reason most crooks rob."

"He wants the money." Piper looked over at Phoebe and Paige. "He needs things, and he's learned enough about how our society operates that he knows he can go buy them."

"What does a demon this powerful need to buy?" Darryl asked.

Piper leaned forward, placing her arms on Darryl's desk. "He's here to create mayhem, to cause the collapse of our society, the way he caused the Greeks to enter their dark ages."

As she spoke, Darryl began writing.

"Get your officers to canvass weapons stores, demolition suppliers—the kinds of places where a survivalist would go shopping," Piper went on.

Paige added to the list. "Check out fertilizer wholesalers, or companies that handle biohazards. He might want to try to start another plague."

"Check out any store where he's been seen,"

added Phoebe. "Maybe we can learn something about where he's going to hit next if we know what he's buying."

"We can saturate the news," said Darryl, "put his picture up, ask for the public's help, but if he taps into the underground market for what he wants, that won't do us any good."

"Right," said Phoebe. "Most illegal weapons dealers aren't likely to come forward and tell you about a sale."

"Then there's that other matter," said Darryl. "What do I tell the officers working on this when they report that this guy is in three different places at the same time?"

Piper sat back. None of the sisters had a suggestion.

"Can we take these things as they come?" asked Phoebe. "Darryl, if you and your officers can keep track of him, can let us know where he's been and what he's buying, we'll work on how to vanquish him."

"Sounds as good as anything I can come up with," said Darryl. "Let's work on stopping him first, and worry about how we explain it later."

The girls stood.

"We also have to keep track of how many times he splits," Piper told Darryl, "so if you hear of any unusual ways of him dying . . ."

"I'll contact you immediately."

Piper sighed. "I guess that's it, then." She started to leave, then turned back. "Can we have copies of where he's been seen, and what he's robbed?"

"Sure." Darryl handed her the copies from his desk. "Take these. I can get more for myself. Any new reports that come in I'll e-mail to you."

"Thanks." She looked around, trying to think of anything else that would be helpful. "We'll work on that plan," she said at last, "and get back to you."

"You do that."

The three left the police station, collected Piper's car from the public lot near the PacBell Building, and drove home.

Leo greeted them when they walked in. "Wyatt and Chase are both sleeping," he said. "You three should get some rest too. It's really late, and you must all be exhausted."

Piper walked over to him, let him wrap his arms around her, and stood, soaking up his embrace for a long moment.

Paige and Phoebe both said good night, and in a moment Piper and Leo were alone. She looked up at him.

"Piper? What is it? You look so . . . sad."

"We almost lost Phoebe," she said. "I know we've been close before, but this time it was so scary. The worst part is that I know there was nothing I could have done in time."

"You needed Paige."

"Yes."

"You need to fight this demon together."

Piper sighed, reluctant to let go of Leo's embrace. "I don't see how we can fight him together when he can be in so many places at once, when there are always so many Innocents to protect." She let Leo guide her to the couch, where they sat down. She continued, "I feel like we should be out there right now."

"You need your rest."

"We need to be fighting him."

"From everything I can tell, this is only going to get worse." Leo smoothed her hair back. "For now, get some sleep. Maybe something will come to you in your dreams."

Leo was quiet for a few minutes, thinking. When he looked down at his wife, Piper was fast asleep.

He carried her to bed.

Piper awoke to the faint sounds of the television coming from the other room. She quickly got up and walked into the living room. Paige sat on the couch, a grocery bag in her hands. She looked back to see Piper. "'Morning," she said. "You slept in your clothes?"

"I don't remember going to sleep." Piper nodded to the TV. "What's our demon up to this morning?"

"Nothing newsworthy," said Paige, "unless he's responsible for the traffic mess on the bridge." She opened the grocery bag. "I went shopping for Chase." She began to take out jars of baby food.

"Hey," Piper said, "peas and carrots. That's what we started Wyatt on."

"I know," said Paige. "I thought I'd try these. Chase needs more than just broth."

"We've got some sweet potatoes," said Piper, sitting down on the couch next to her. "Wyatt loves mashed sweet potatoes."

"Okay, I'll try that, too." Paige looked over at her sister. "You know, caring for Chase, when he's so . . . helpless . . . has really given me a different understanding of what taking care of a baby is like."

"I'll bet."

"I mean, I'm crazy about Wyatt, and you know I love to do things with him, but at the end of the day I give him back to you, or to Leo." She sighed. "Chase feels more—I don't know, more mine. My responsibility. And that really makes a difference."

"You care about him, don't you?"

Paige smiled. "It must have been so obvious. I mean, I spent all that time boning up on all things Greek, and most of it was just so I could have an excuse to spend more time with him."

"Well, it worked."

"Yeah. And now, he's here, in our house, and I can spend all the time with him I want, washing him, feeding him, talking to him . . . and there's nothing he can do for me. So it's not about me getting something out of it. It's just . . ."

"I know," said Piper. "It *is* like having a baby."

"Except Wyatt never needs a shave."

Piper smiled. "Are you going to try that today?"

"I think so. Chase *is* getting a little scraggly."

"Good luck." Piper looked around. "Where's Phoebe?"

"She went to her office. Wanted to make an early, quick appearance while things were quiet."

Piper groaned. "I didn't even call P3 last night. Don't think it even crossed my mind."

"Hey, you were busy." Paige cocked her head. "Why not call that bartender, the one who puts his own money in the till?"

"Bernie."

"Yeah. Him. Tell him you're so impressed, you're going to let him look after things for a few days."

"That," said Piper, "is a great idea." She got up, moving toward the kitchen. "Holler if our demon shows up on the morning news. I'm going to put breakfast on."

"Take a shower first. Get into a change of clothes. I think you'll feel better."

Piper glanced at the news. Still only stock market quotes and traffic reports. "Okay. I guess I have time for that."

Phoebe came in as Piper put the eggs and toast on the table. Over breakfast, the Charmed Ones laid out a strategy.

"We know what he's really after," said Piper.

"At least, I hope we do. He's going to create mayhem, forcing us, and the police, and different shop owners, to try to stop him. And after we've used every way we can think of to kill him, he'll have an army."

"An army that we won't know how to defeat," Paige added.

Piper continued her point. "So, killing him—with guns, knives, swords, or explosions—won't work."

Phoebe chimed in. "So far, that's exactly what we've been doing."

"Which is why," Piper said, "we've got to come up with something else."

"We can't very well just let him run amok," said Phoebe.

"No," said Piper. "We have to outsmart him. Now. Before he gets that army of his."

Paige pushed away her plate. "Any ideas?"

"I want to go back to the Book of Shadows," Piper said. "It's never let us down before. Which means, I think, that we've been asking the wrong questions."

"Sounds good," said Paige. "What do you think Phoebe and I should do?"

"Keep an eye on him—them. Keep as many Innocents safe as you can." Piper took from her pocket the three potions she'd made up the day before. "We haven't tried these yet. If you get the chance, see what happens. Maybe this third one will send a copy of him back to the netherworld."

"Every little bit helps," said Phoebe, picking up the potions. "If we could vanquish even a few of them, it would have to make things easier." She stood. "I want to hold the demon egg again, see if I can get any more visions of where he might be."

"Don't do that alone," said Piper. "The last time, it really took a toll on you."

"I won't."

"Let's all go up to the attic," said Paige. "I can check in on Chase, Piper can look in the Book, and Phoebe, you can see what you see in the egg."

The three sisters checked in on Chase first. He appeared to be sleeping.

"You're right about his needing a shave," whispered Piper.

Phoebe crinkled her nose. "Um, from that smell, I'd say he needs more than a shave. He needs a bath."

Paige's mouth dropped open. "I can't bathe him," she said. "He's not even my boyfriend."

Piper arched an eyebrow. "Oh, because I'm the mom here, I should do it?"

"Maybe we should all do it together," said Phoebe. "I mean, he's big—it would be hard for any one of us to do."

Paige looked uncertain. "Won't this be . . . weird?"

"No," Piper said matter-of-factly, "and here's why. All kinds of adults need help like this. Grown children do this for their aged parents when they can't take care of themselves anymore. Spouses do this for their husbands or wives, when they're stricken with cancer or with some other debilitating disease. This is what people do, every day, when it has to be done."

"Right," said Paige. "Of course." She nodded. "I'll go get some clean sheets."

"And bring a washcloth, some soap, and some warm water." Piper looked at Phoebe. "Let's get started."

After Chase was bathed and his sheets were changed, Piper went to the Book. Paige sat next to Chase, a razor and some shaving cream in her hand. She saw that he was awake. "Let's get you shaved."

She smoothed his face with warm water, then rubbed the shaving cream into a lather and applied it to his beard a little at a time. She picked up the razor, uncertain. She glanced at him, watched him watching her. "Okay," she said, "I'm going to guess that this is like shaving my legs, only hairier and bumpier." She took a breath. "Here goes."

Little by little, she shaved his cheek, his neck, his chin, growing more confident in her ability as she went on. She carefully wiped the shaving cream away and tracked down any errant drips of water before they could slide onto his chest. When she looked at him, those green eyes were closely following her moves. It seemed they were smiling again.

As she worked, she glanced from time to time at Piper, who stood over the Book of Shadows, thoughtfully reading page after page. Piper closed the Book just as Paige was wiping the last of the shaving cream away. "You rest now," Paige said to Chase. "I'll be back with something to eat soon."

She moved over to Phoebe, who stood near the egg, holding her hand close to it but not touching it. Phoebe pulled her hand back, looking at Paige. "I wish we could carry this downstairs. I don't want to . . . explore it . . . so close to—" She spoke softly, nodding back to Chase.

"We can't move him, either," said Paige. "He and the egg are a package deal now."

"Let's let Phoebe hold the egg here." Piper looked at her sisters. "He's already seen enough to know something very weird is going on."

"Well," said Phoebe, "he's about to see a little more."

"Not *here* here," said Piper. She picked up the egg halves and motioned to Paige and Phoebe to follow her into the corner of the attic behind Grams's old dresser. "Is he okay if the egg is this far away?"

Paige checked. "He seems to be."

Piper turned to Phoebe. "At least this dresser will shield you from him a little bit."

Phoebe motioned for Piper to give her the egg.

"Better sit down first," Piper warned.

Phoebe sat, composed herself, then nodded.

Piper sat near her, slowly holding out both halves of the egg, one in each hand. Phoebe moved her hands closer, one hovering over each half of the egg. Slowly, slowly, she lowered her hands until she lightly made contact.

Phoebe's body immediately jolted. She stiffened, her eyes rolled back, and she began to tremble violently all over. She opened her mouth to speak, but no words came out.

Piper gasped. "Paige! Help me pull them away!"

Paige reached out, but the egg was welded to Phoebe's hands. Together, Piper and Paige managed to yank the halves from Phoebe's grasp.

Phoebe shot backward, landing hard against the attic wall. She gasped, looking at her hands, which appeared gnarled and arthritic.

Paige laid the halves of the egg down, and both she and Piper embraced Phoebe, holding her tightly and gently massaging her hands.

Gradually, Phoebe returned to normal. She sat, blinking, staring at the floor.

"How bad is it going to be?" asked Piper.

Phoebe tried to speak. Her mouth trembled, and a tear ran down her cheek. "I can do this," she reassured herself.

"Take your time," Piper cooed. "No rush. Find a place to start. Something that isn't the worst."

"There isn't any part that's not really, really

awful." Phoebe closed her eyes and took a deep breath. "It was like a hundred movies, all going at once, all running in fast motion." After a moment, she went on. "More killings, more savagery. Then the demons started moving in packs. Two, then three, then more. Creating terror. And then"—she looked up at Piper—"a wasteland. It was San Francisco, I could tell, but it was . . . whole blocks leveled . . . fires . . . people trying to flee. . . ." She shook her head. "It looked like, I don't know, like the pictures I've seen of Dresden, during World War Two, when the whole city had been bombed." She paused. "And the demons were in a line, coming through the ruins, carrying these big swords and looking for anyone who was still alive."

The three of them sat in the corner of the attic, holding one another and rocking softly.

Chapter Ten

Phoebe's words echoed in Piper's brain as they sat together in the attic. "We can't allow that to happen," she said finally. "We must not allow that level of destruction, no matter what it takes." She turned to Phoebe. "I'm going to make you a broth," she said, "a calming broth. I want you to try to recall any specifics from those images that you think might help us, but only after you've had the broth."

"We don't have time for that," said Phoebe. She began to stand. "It's only an image. I can—" She wobbled on her feet.

Piper helped her sit back down. "I've never seen you react like this to a vision. I'm going to make the broth, and you're going to rest here and think about bunnies or kittens or something pleasant until I get back."

Phoebe didn't argue. She sat back against the attic wall. Paige covered her with a blanket, then sat next to her as Piper went down to the kitchen. Paige began to hum a lullaby, and soon Phoebe nestled her head in Paige's lap.

Piper came back a few minutes later, a steaming bowl of broth in her hands.

Phoebe sat up, took the bowl, and slowly sipped a little. "Thanks," she said, "both of you. I feel better now."

"Finish the broth," ordered Piper. "Then we'll talk."

Phoebe sipped some more. "This is good," she said. "What's in it?"

"You might not want to know."

Phoebe smiled. "Funny, but hearing you say that doesn't bother me at all."

"Good. Then the broth is working."

Piper waited until Phoebe had finished the broth, then went on. "Now," she said gently, "forget the horror. The mayhem. The suffering. See the demons again. How are they doing the things they're doing? How are they multiplying so quickly?

"The army," said Phoebe. "Our army. The military. Tanks. Flame-throwers. Air strikes will hit several demons working together, and multiply all of them."

"That makes sense," said Piper. "The more force we use, the more the demon multiplies, and then the more force we have to use the next time."

Paige piped up. "Our own forces must destroy a lot of San Francisco."

"And by then," Phoebe added, "we know we're dealing with something not of this world, and panic sets in."

"Which is, I imagine, exactly what he wants." Piper looked grim.

"Okay," said Paige. "I think we can use this."

"What are you thinking?" asked Piper.

"He's lying low for now. He's biding his time, getting ready. But when that happens, when he's ready to move, he'll want panic, like Phoebe just said. He'll want rumors of what a beast he is. He'll want publicity." Paige looked at her sisters. "Let's make sure he doesn't get it."

"Sounds good," said Phoebe, "except how do we do that?"

"We keep the press out of this." Paige looked at Piper. "We tell Darryl not to issue any releases. They do that kind of thing with serial killers when they don't want the public to know everything."

"So he doesn't get publicity," said Phoebe. "He's still out there creating mayhem."

"The longer we keep the army out of this," said Piper, "the longer it is before they try using more force to stop him."

"Then we hunt the demons down now," said Paige, "and stop them before they really get started."

"I've got some locations for us to try," said Phoebe. "Lots of them, actually." She reached for a pen and paper. "Let me write down a few, and we can get started on thwarting him."

As Phoebe wrote, Piper went to the Book and Paige walked over to Chase.

"Hey," Paige said softly. "How much of that did you hear?"

His eyes watched her, unblinking.

"Right. Yes or no questions. Did you understand what we're talking about?"

Chase blinked once, slowly.

"Maybe you think you understand a little?"

He blinked twice.

"But what you understand makes no sense to you?"

He blinked twice again.

"Yeah, we get that a lot." She looked over at her sisters. "We're witches. Good witches. And we're here to fight the evil that walks the earth. Evil that most people aren't even aware of." She thought for a moment. "Just like most tourists aren't aware of the power of the ocean."

Understanding flooded Chase's eyes.

"Yeah. Thought that would make sense to you. Some people see the forces that shape the weather, the climate, and understand why it's freezing here on a day in June. Others . . . well, others never think about things like that, so they go through life unaware of such forces."

Chase watched her intently, waiting.

"Right now, my sisters and I are on one side of this, and that thing that came out of the dragon's egg is on the other." She paused. "And

you, Chase . . . you're caught in the middle."
Paige forced a smile. "At least until we get
things straightened out." She smoothed the
blanket, pulling it up over his shoulders. "So
hang in there. When we're finished with that
guy and his friends who look like you, we'll get
you back to normal."

Chase blinked twice.

"Good." She glanced over at her sisters. Piper
closed the Book, and Phoebe finished her list,
looking up at Paige. "Gotta go," Paige said to
Chase. "But I'll be back."

The three sisters left the attic.

When they got downstairs, Leo was feeding
Wyatt, who was strapped into his high chair.

"Hey," said Piper, walking up to Wyatt, "there's
my big boy."

Wyatt gurgled, holding out a hand toward
Piper.

Piper touched his hand, letting Wyatt wrap
his tiny fingers around her pinkie.

"Mommy and aunties have a bad ol' demon
to go and fight." She stroked the back of his fingers gently. "You probably know all about that."
She leaned over and kissed him. "Anyway, be a
good boy for Daddy, and Mommy will be back
soon." She looked at Leo. "This one's going to be
even tougher than we thought," she said, "but
we've got to get it right."

"Isn't that always the case?" he asked.

"Never more than this time." She kissed him

softly. "I'll fill you in tonight. Right now, we're going to try to reduce the demon's numbers, if we can."

"Good luck."

Piper turned to Phoebe. "Okay," she said, "I want three birds, one stone. Pick a place where we can save an Innocent, keep Green Eyes out of the press, and maybe reduce his number by one."

Phoebe consulted her list. "Here's one," she said. "The demon is strangling a woman in an apartment in Haight-Ashbury when her husband comes in, blows him away with a shotgun."

Piper looked surprised. "What, nobody has done that yet?"

"Guess not. According to the movie version in my head, the demon splits, then kills both the wife and the husband."

"I can see why the press would be all over that one," said Paige. "Sounds smarmy. When?"

Phoebe walked to the window and looked at the sun. "About . . . now, I'm guessing."

Piper picked up her car keys. "Let's go."

The three parked across from Haight Street, near the corner of Buena Vista Park. They cut across the park, startling a homeless man.

"It's all right," Paige assured him, "we're here to help."

"Social workers," grumbled the man. He moved to the other side of the park.

Phoebe looked at the apartments across the street. "This looks right," she said. She scanned the street, then saw a woman struggling to get a large bundle of dry cleaning out of her car. A man who looked like Chase, but dressed differently, stopped and offered to help.

"Clever," observed Piper. "He knows to dump those clothes that have been seen on TV."

"How do we want to do this?" asked Phoebe. "Waiting until they get inside makes no sense."

"I say we freeze the girl and blow him up."

Piper looked at Paige, surprised. "Here? On the street? We're trying to *lower* his public profile, remember?"

"Whatever we do, we'd better do it fast," said Phoebe. "They're almost to her apartment building."

The three began to cross the street. "Okay," said Piper, "I'll freeze the girl. Paige, you orb us and the demon into the park. We can vanquish him there."

The three approached the couple. The demon, carrying the heavy bundle of clothes, said something that made the woman laugh.

They moved closer until they were right behind the couple. The demon looked over his shoulder, recognizing them.

"Now!" said Paige.

Piper froze the woman as Paige reached out and touched the demon's sleeve, orbing the four of them across the street.

As soon as they appeared in the park, Piper gestured, and the demon exploded.

"So far, so good," said Paige.

As they watched, shattered bits of demon began to gather into two piles, forming bodies, limbs.

Piper pulled the third potion out of her pocket, reciting as she did so:

> *Demon from an ancient realm,*
> *Go back from whence you came.*
> *You are not dead, but in death's stead,*
> *You're banished, just the same.*

Piper flung the potion at the reassembling piles.

A vortex appeared, looking like a small gray tornado. It vacuumed up the bits of exploded demon that were quickly forming into two new bodies, the vortex turning blacker as it did so.

"That's kind of . . . small . . . for a vortex," said Paige.

"Gee, I'll remember that for next time," said Piper.

Paige glanced around the park, looking for the homeless man or anyone else who might see what they were doing. "Is it supposed to take this long?"

"I don't know," said Piper. "I've never done one quite like this."

The vortex, completely black now, began to

sink into the ground. As it did so, a hand came out, grasping a branch of a bush next to the leading edge of the whirling funnel cloud. Phoebe watched, horrified. "Piper?"

A head appeared, then two arms. The demon struggled to pull itself out of the swirling debris field. He looked at them and smiled.

Phoebe leaped forward, catching the demon's head with a roundhouse karate kick. The head disappeared, along with one hand, but the other, the hand holding the branches, hung on. "Blow him up again!" Phoebe shouted, kicking again at the hand.

"I can't!" said Piper. "It won't work on him twice!"

Phoebe kicked the branch, snapping it off, and the hand disappeared.

The vortex sank completely into the earth.

"That was close," said Paige.

Phoebe looked across the park. "Piper, the frozen woman."

Piper turned, gestured, and the woman nearly collapsed under the weight of her dry cleaning. The clothes tumbled to the sidewalk, and she looked around, confused.

The three sisters sat down on the grass, out of sight. "Give her a minute," said Piper. "Let's hope she goes in and tells her husband . . ." She trailed off. "Right now, I don't care what she tells her husband, as long as the two of them are safe."

"Score one for us," said Phoebe. "Two Innocents saved, and one bad guy who didn't get to multiply."

"One bad guy who's gone," added Paige. "One we can scratch off the list."

"But at what cost?" Piper looked at her sisters. "Now I can't blow them up."

"But we didn't kill him," Paige reminded her, "we just banished him. So sending them into a vortex should still work next time."

"Except that this time, we shattered him to pieces," Phoebe added, "and he still didn't flush."

Paige looked over to where the woman struggled with her dry cleaning, finally getting it inside her building. "We know this demon is going to be hard to stop," she said. "But we also know that the more we can contain him now, the better. I say we count any victory as a good thing, and move on."

Her sisters nodded.

Behind them, they heard the homeless guy scream. The three sisters leaped to their feet, running in his direction.

Across the park they saw the vortex, larger this time, rising out of the ground and whirling next to the vagabond, who shielded his eyes from the force of blowing debris.

"That vortex is reversed," Piper yelled. "It's blowing *out*."

As they watched, four demons emerged from

the whirling vortex just before it disappeared.

The sisters stopped, dumbstruck.

The demons walked quickly toward the edge of the park. One turned, raising an arm in their direction in a kind of greeting or salute.

"Thank . . . you," the sisters heard him call.

The four demons broke into a trot down the street.

Chapter Eleven

Piper, Paige, and Phoebe returned to the Manor, feeling very down.

"We've got to do something," said Phoebe. "They didn't break up and go in different directions this time. They stayed as a pack. It could be starting."

"What could be starting?" Paige asked.

"The destruction that I saw."

"Give me a minute," said Piper. "Just . . . a minute. Or two. I want to talk to Leo alone."

Piper went into Wyatt's room, checking on him. He was asleep in his crib. She brushed the side of his face, then walked out and found Leo in the kitchen. He sat with Piper's demon list. Piper, reading over his shoulder, could see that he'd added three demons to the list, that now the total was up to nine.

"So," she said, pulling him up and out of his chair, "you already know what happened."

Leo nodded.

She led him into their bedroom, closed the door, and rested her head on his shoulder. "Please tell me what happened." Before he could speak, she went on. "We gave it our best shot. I *know* I used a spell that didn't kill him. Them. It should have worked."

"When you blew him up, he died. And was splitting when you vacuumed him to the Underworld."

"Still, he—they—were gone. Not dead, just gone."

"The problem is that you didn't account for what can happen in the Underworld."

Piper lifted her head off his shoulder, staring at him, trying to make sense of this. "They got themselves killed in the Underworld?"

"It's possible," said Leo. "Only, with these demons, that gave them the chance to come back here."

"That is so not fair," said Piper. "If they get killed in the Underworld, they should have to stay in the Underworld."

"This is an ancient and very powerful demon. Something is keeping them all together. Some bond. You're going to have to factor that into your thinking."

"Oh, Leo . . . ," she felt like punching him, or crying, or both. "I need help here. I'm in over my head. All of our powers seem useless against this one." She gave up the idea of punching him and settled against his chest. "We can't kill him. Now we can't even banish him. And protecting Innocents, by stopping him for the moment, only makes him stronger." She let out a heavy sigh. "Phoebe has seen the total destruction of San Francisco. Like the whole city had been bombed. And I don't know how to stop that from happening."

Leo wrapped his arm around her, holding her. "You need some rest."

"No!" she said, pulling away. "I need some answers! I *need* some help! I've got to get back out there, *now*, and stop this thing!"

"Shhhh . . ." Leo pulled her back against his chest. "What you're doing isn't working. What you want to do will only make things worse, will only make him stronger. You need to let go of that."

"This is helpful?" She glared at him. "Telling me it's hopeless—*this* is how you help me?"

"I didn't say it was hopeless. Relax, Piper. Listen."

She realized that her chest was heaving, as if she'd run a mile. She took a deep breath, willing herself to calm down. "Okay," she said, "I'm listening."

"Close your eyes and picture something for me."

She closed her eyes, waiting.

"If you were trying to catch a frightened bird that got into the house—"

"Leo, this is not some frightened bird! This is a demon about to lay waste to the whole city!"

"Piper . . ."

That one word carried many messages. It was gentle, it was reassuring, and it transported just a hint that Leo was about to lose patience with her.

"Right," she said. "Calm." She took a deep breath and let it out. "I'm calm now." She closed her eyes again. "There's some little bird loose in the house, destroying the entire city—"

"*Piper . . .*" Leo's warning was stronger this time.

She sighed. "Okay. I'm with you. There's a bird in the house."

"He's frightened. And the more you try to catch him, the more frightened he becomes. Now he's beginning to bang into things, frantic to get out."

"I'm with you," she said. "I see it."

"Good. What do you do?"

"I step back. I let him calm down."

"Good."

"Except if I step back from this demon—"

"The bird, Piper. Stay with the bird. Forget the demon, for just one minute."

She rubbed her forehead, but kept her eyes closed. After a moment, she folded both hands back into her lap. "Okay. He's frightened. I step back."

"Now what happens?"

"I think of ways to get him out without frightening him again."

"Good. What are they?"

"I could . . . open a window and wait."

"Or?"

"I could . . . open a door. And wait."

"Anything else?"

"No. That's about it."

"Why?"

"Because he can't stay in the house. And the more I chase him, the more he just flies around. So I need to coax him to . . ." She stopped, opening her eyes, staring into Leo's. "Ohhh . . . I see it now."

"What do you see?"

"It's just like your bird. I can't destroy him. Instead, I need to get him to go back to where he came from."

"Yes." Leo nodded. "Put him back in the egg. You're right. That could work."

"Yeah, like you didn't know that all along. Why not just tell me?"

"Because I didn't think of it."

"What? That whole bird thing—you didn't know what I would say?"

He shook his head. "I just wanted you to come at this from a different angle."

"Wow." Piper considered this for a moment. "Cosmic."

"Yeah."

She sighed. "But I can't leave the demon alone, like I did the bird."

"No, but you might be able to lull him."

"Maybe. Or maybe not. The biggest difference between your bird and the demon is that the demon is bent on destruction." She stood up. "Maybe it would have been a better analogy if you'd told me we had an alligator in the house. Or a bull in a china shop."

"No, because then you would have thought of vanquishing the alligator, or the bull."

"You're probably right." Piper went back to the problem at hand. "What the bird and the demon have in common is that we want to get them both to go back to where they came from. I want the bird to be outside again, and I want that demon back in his egg again."

Leo stood up beside her, and she kissed him softly. "Thank you," she said.

"Glad I could help," he said. "I know how hard this one has been."

"Yeah, and it's not over yet." Piper moved to the door, then turned back to him. "I know now that we want that thing back in his egg, but I have no idea how we're going to do that."

Chapter Twelve

Piper sat with Phoebe and Paige in the kitchen and told them about her conversation with Leo. "Maybe," she concluded, "we can figure out how to get all the demon versions of Chase back into that egg."

"I'm worried most about that newest demon pack," said Phoebe. "They've just been to the Underworld, and they stayed together when they left the park."

"Do you think you can track them?" asked Piper.

"I could try picking up a vision at the park."

"I don't like that idea," said Piper. "Your visions are getting more violent, and you seem to be more affected by them."

Paige looked at her. "I've been getting these strange . . . vibes . . . since that thing got out yesterday. I'm sure they're coming from the demons. Or from the Innocents they threaten. Maybe we can track them if I orb to those energy readings."

Piper nodded. "If those last four are still in a pack, then they should be giving you the strongest reading."

"I think the three of us should track them," said Paige, "see what they're up to."

"Take Phoebe with you," said Piper. "I'm going to check the Book. Maybe there's a way to lull a demon. Maybe we can do something similar to letting that poor little bird calm down."

"Then it's a date," said Paige. "Phoebe and I'll see what he's up to. You'll figure out how to slip him a Mickey."

"Whoa," said Piper. "'Slip him a Mickey.' There's a saying I haven't heard since Grams was around."

Phoebe stood up. "Maybe some of Grams's thinking is just what we need right now."

"Let's do it," said Paige. She reached for Phoebe's hand and orbed them away.

Piper went up to the attic. She checked in on Chase, made sure he was comfortable, then moved to the Book of Shadows. She opened it, smoothed its pages, and concentrated on finding something that would help calm a demon.

She began to turn the pages, pausing at last when she found what looked to be a relevant charm.

Plant a garden filled with these:
Mugwort, moonwort, madwort three.
Boil three score of young, fresh leaves
Then brew a potion, sure to please
The heart of any demon man.
Of this potion, let him sup
Until he's drained his wassail cup.
Then let him sleep, perchance to dream
Of kinder times than now they seem.
If this can't lull him, nothing can.

Piper was both pleased and troubled as she read this. Pleased because they were definitely dealing with a manlike demon. Troubled because she had no time to plant a garden and let it grow until she could be harvesting leaves twenty at a time. Pleased because the idea of putting the demons to sleep seemed as if it would give them the break they were looking for. Troubled because the last line of the charm was so ominous, seeming to imply that failure was, in fact, an option.

"First things first," she said to herself. She needed to find a garden ready to harvest now. She hoped it wouldn't matter that she hadn't planted it herself, as the charm suggested. She went downstairs, turned on her computer, and began to search the Internet.

Paige and Phoebe orbed into an alley and landed in a smelly Dumpster.

"Okay," said Phoebe, climbing out and moving away from the stench, "why did you pick this alley?"

"This is the strongest reading I got," said Paige. "Although I have to tell you, there were plenty to choose from."

"He's getting ready to make his move," said Phoebe. "That's why you're getting so many readings. Let's hope Piper comes up with that spell."

They walked out of the alleyway to see several police cruisers surrounding a building. Phoebe and Paige saw Darryl half crouched behind his car, and they crossed over to him.

"What's up?" asked Phoebe.

Darryl turned, startled to see them. "How did you know where to find me? We worked hard to keep the press out of this one."

"We're tracking the demon, not you," said Paige.

"Oh." He turned back to look at the building. "I'm glad to see you, but I don't think you can help on this one."

Phoebe scanned the building, looking for signs of trouble. "What is it?"

"Hostage situation." Darryl nodded at the building. "A gang of four has taken over the savings and loan on the first floor over there. We think there are twenty-two people in there with them."

"Twenty-two . . . ," Phoebe nearly whispered

the number. "Darryl, the four are our newest
pack of demons. They won't care about the
people. They'll only care about getting killed in
a way that hasn't been done before. If your men
move in, it's going to be a bloodbath."

"You might be right," said Darryl. He looked
tired. "We got a call from one of the women
inside. She said they were being taken hostage
by quadruplets. That's about all she could tell us
before the line went dead."

Paige nodded solemnly at Phoebe. "You were
right," she said. "This sounds like he's raising
the stakes."

"He's been pretty quiet until now," Phoebe
said. She looked at Darryl. "But now, he's going
to want the publicity. He wants us to panic. The
four of them will die in some big, bloody way,
and then they'll come back on a rampage and
we'll increase our violence in trying to stop
them. We'll start to destroy San Francisco in
order to save it." She stopped. Practically pleading, she added, "You can't storm the building.
That'll be what he wants."

"If he starts killing hostages, that's exactly
what we'll do. But it won't be my call." He nodded to the head of the SWAT team, setting up a
command post behind an armored truck. "It'll
be his."

Phoebe looked to Paige. "This is up to us,"
she said. "We need to get those people out of
there before they start to die."

"What should I do, orb in and take them out one by one?"

"Yes!" said Phoebe. "Great idea."

"Wait, I was being sarcastic." Paige looked at the building, then looked back at Phoebe. "Do you really think I should orb in, grab somebody, and orb back out?"

Darryl chimed in, "The demons already know you two, right?"

"Yes," said Phoebe, "we've met. Some of them, anyway." She looked at Darryl. "We're still not sure if that's the same thing or not."

"So instead of orbing a bunch of ordinary citizens who have no idea who you are . . ."

"We orb the bad guys?" Paige looked thoughtful. "That might work."

Phoebe didn't feel so sure. "What do we know about them? How are they armed? Where are they? Are they together? Are they scattered among the hostages? How does she get from one to the other? What happens if she orbs one out and the others notice?"

Darryl held up his hand as if to stop her from talking anymore. "Good questions," he said. "Let's see how many we can answer." He crossed carefully toward the command post.

Phoebe and Paige glanced at each other, then followed. When they got close, they could see that the SWAT team leader had spread a floor plan over a car's trunk and was showing it to Darryl. As Phoebe and Paige got closer, the leader glanced suspiciously at them. "Who are the civilians?" he asked.

"A psychic I've worked with before," said Darryl, "and her sister." He turned to Phoebe and Paige. "This is Captain Rodgers."

Captain Rodgers looked unimpressed. "I've got no time for a psychic to tell me what I already know. Four perps are holding a lot of people hostage. I'm going in. I'm not waiting until people are already dead."

Darryl held the captain's gaze. "I've seen her do some pretty amazing things. If she can help us avoid any bloodshed, I'd like to give her a chance."

Rodgers looked from the sisters back to Darryl. "When we're ready, I'm going in. You've got about five minutes."

Darryl nodded, took the floor plan, and stepped away from the command post, out of earshot of Rodgers, who went back to planning, ignoring them.

Darryl moved the sisters back out of the way behind his car, where they could talk in private. Phoebe noticed that no one paid them any attention. Everyone was focused on the building.

"There's a back door behind the counter, in the corner," Darryl said, pointing at the schematic. "This is the vault. There are three desks across from the counter, and an office in the near corner." He let the sisters study the map a moment. "They pulled the blinds, but Rodgers has officers listening on high-tech equipment. He says the hostages are here"—he pointed to an area between the vault and the desks—"down on the floor, all huddled together."

"Why is the captain going in so soon?" Paige asked.

"The officers who are listening told him the four plan to start killing the hostages. Soon."

Paige looked over at the front of the savings and loan. "Have they made any demands?"

"No. That's why he wants to go in now. If we had demands, somebody could be negotiating. Without that, Captain Rodgers has few choices."

"Let me slip into the back of that group of hostages," Paige said, pointing at the floor plan. "I can check out where the demons are standing, then orb back out, and we can decide where you want me to put them."

"What if one of them sees you?" asked Darryl.

Paige looked him in the eye. "What happens if I don't go in?"

"I'll see about a secure area around here," Darryl replied. "You slip in and take a look around."

Paige nodded, then orbed away.

When she was gone, Phoebe laid a gentle hand on Darryl's shoulder. "I know you're used to giving orders in a situation like this," she said. "But you have to let us do what we think best now. You have to let us do what we do."

Darryl sighed, looking out over the squad cars, at the officers behind them, and the building. "I understand," he said. "But this is my world here. I need some kind of control."

"You're not going to get it with this demon." Phoebe followed his gaze over the scene. "You're in control of your officers here. We'll go after the demon. Just think of it as us working side by side."

Darryl nodded. "I can do that."

Paige orbed back next to them.

"Did anybody see you?" asked Phoebe.

"Nobody even noticed. They're all too terrified." She looked at Darryl, pointing at the blueprint of the building. "You were right. The hostages are all here." She tapped the space in front of the vault with her finger. "They're lying facedown, most of them not moving. They're really scared." She moved her finger across to the customer service counter. "The demons are here."

"All four of them?" asked Darryl.

Paige nodded. "They're all armed. All standing there, side by side. They look like they're waiting for something."

"They're waiting to be attacked," said Phoebe. "That's why they're in the building in the first place." She pointed to the counter on the blueprint. "Paige, can you orb back in behind this? Grab one or two and orb out?"

"I think I can do better," said Paige. "I can orb back *onto* the counter, reach out and touch all four with an arm, or a leg . . . or some part of me, and orb them all out together."

Darryl watched as Rodgers began to signal to his officers on the roof, on the sidewalk next to the front doors.

Phoebe noticed the activity too. "Do it," she said. She looked at Darryl. "And she'll bring them . . . where?"

Darryl glanced around quickly. "Inside the armored truck?"

Phoebe watched as the SWAT team members on the sidewalk prepared to rush the door. "Is anyone in that armored truck?"

Darryl ran to the back of the truck, opened the door, looked inside, closed the door, and turned to Phoebe, shaking his head.

"Lock the door," Phoebe said.

Darryl did.

Phoebe turned to Paige. "Now," she ordered.

Paige orbed away. A second later, the SWAT team burst through the doors of the building.

Phoebe could hear the shouting and confusion coming from inside the building. People began to scream, but no shots were fired.

Paige orbed back beside her. "Done," she said. "All four demons are in the big, hunky truck now." She paused. "Of course, they're still armed."

The sound of muffled gunfire caught everyone's attention. The bulletproof glass of the armored car spidered, but held. Darryl and the officers who were left on the street turned to the vehicle, the officers staring open-mouthed as cries and screams and curses came from inside the truck, along with more gunfire.

Darryl walked back to the sisters. "Good work," he said. He nodded to the front doors of the bank, where the SWAT team was exiting with hostages.

Phoebe saw Captain Rodgers motioning to several of his armed men. They were preparing to open the back of the truck and fire into it. "No," she said, turning to Darryl. "They can't open the back of that truck. The minute they do, the demons get out, and we start all over."

Before Darryl could react, the engine of the truck turned over, then rumbled to life.

Paige looked at Phoebe, astonished. "When did they learn how to drive?"

The truck careened down the street, smashing into a row of parked cars on one side before veering across to smash into several cars on the other side.

"Apparently," Phoebe replied dryly, "they haven't yet."

Captain Rodgers ordered his SWAT team to fire at the tires, but the truck kept rumbling down the boulevard.

A SWAT team member with a bazooka took aim and fired. The shell hit the back of the truck, breaking its axle, and the truck flipped onto its side and skidded to a stop.

The SWAT team approached, advancing from parked car to parked car, weapons ready. They were about a block from the wreckage when the front passenger door of the upended truck flipped open and demons began to climb out and down to the street.

The SWAT team opened fire on the demons. Some fired back as they continued to clamber out and flee.

Paige counted as they climbed out, ducking as shots were fired, then looking back up. "Six . . . seven . . . eight . . ." She glanced at Phoebe. "Four went in, eight came out."

Phoebe made notes. "Do we call that death by traffic accident, or death by bazooka?"

Paige shook her head. "Not sure." She looked over at Darryl, who was listening to the two of them with his mouth slightly hanging open. "I'd suggest telling Captain Rodgers that you believe they have a new, lightweight form of body armor." She looked back down the street, where SWAT members ran after the demons, who had by now disappeared. "And I guess you'd better tell him that everybody miscalculated on how many of them there were."

"And what do I tell him," asked Darryl, "when he wants to know how they got out of the bank and into the truck in the first place?"

Paige looked at Phoebe, then back at Darryl. "We'll let you handle that one," she said.

"How many of them are there now?" he asked.

"Thirteen." Phoebe held up her notepad. "At least, thirteen that we know about." She sighed. "This is where it starts to get *really* bad. This is the beginning of what I saw in my vision. Captain Rodgers will certainly hunt some of them down, destroying several in new ways, multiplying them. And when he realizes he can't stop them, he'll call in the army, who will kill more of them in packs, like what just happened here. And we'll go from thirteen to twenty-six to fifty-two in a big hurry." She placed a hand on Darryl's shoulder. "Remember, we're dealing with a demon that loves to die."

The three of them looked out over the city. Paige wondered how long it would be before the skyline was filled with smoke and flames.

Chapter Thirteen

Piper entered the Enchanted Garden plant store and looked around.

Sun filtered in through skylights, illuminating the smooth-pebbled path that curved from the front door to the back of the shop. Plants covered every surface, and the sound of running water emanated from a dozen small fountains. Lawn gnomes, ceramic frogs, and wood-carved toadstools peeked out from under many of the potted bushes that lined the path.

Piper closed the door, causing the small bell attached to the top of the doorsill to ring. A woman appeared from the back room, looking like a character from a Dickens novel. She was short, with gray hair pulled into a bun, and she wore a dark wool shawl over her gray, shapeless dress.

The woman smiled. "Hello, dear, what can I do for you?"

°   "Are you Mrs. Pickens?" Piper asked.

"Please," said the woman, "call me Emily."

"I went to your Web site," Piper said. "It says you carry exotic herbs and medicinals." She walked farther into the shop, following the winding path toward the counter at the back, where Emily stood. The counter, Piper realized, was one large slab from a tree, its bark-covered sides making it look almost as if it could still be alive.

"We carry quite a few. Our specialty, in fact." Emily nodded to the more common plants along the path. "These keep us in business, though. Not much call anymore for the healing herbs."

Piper took a list out of her pocket. "I'm look-ing for mugwort, moonwort, and madwort."

"Ah," said Emily, a keener interest moving across her face. "Casting a spell, are we?"

"I'm just . . . starting a garden."

Emily nodded. "We have those. In the back."

Piper followed Emily through a door behind the counter. They crossed through a small, clut-tered storage room and entered a large garden behind it. Piper looked around, surprised. "Wow, you have so much space back here."

"Yes, we're lucky that way. The shop and this land have been in my family for generations. The city's sort of grown up around us."

The ground was covered in a rich, peaty earth. Dozens—perhaps hundreds—of plants in pots were scattered over the land. Overhead, netting filtered out the harshest of the sun's rays.

"Over here."

Piper turned to see Emily standing in a group of small, potted plants. She walked over to her.

"Now, dear, how soon do you wish to cast this spell?"

"I'm sorry?"

Emily considered, then tried again. "How big do you need your plants to be?"

"Um . . ." Piper debated how much to reveal. "I need twenty leaves each."

Emily's hand went to her chest. "Twenty . . . you must be casting a very powerful spell."

"Can we leave spells out of this? Please? I need some plants."

"Of course."

Emily turned, considering. She pulled a hand cart closer to her, then proceeded to place several plants on it, separating them into three sections.

Piper watched her. Emily was carefully picking out four or five plants of each kind, and each plant had, Piper guessed, at least twenty leaves on it. "I don't think I need nearly that many," she said.

Emily turned back to her. "You want twenty leaves each for your—your garden."

Piper nodded.

"But you don't want just any leaves." Emily held up one of the plants, fingering the leaves carefully. "See here? These longer leaves are slightly darker, thicker. . . ." She shook her head. "That's not what you want."

"No?"

"No. You want these." Emily touched another leaf, which was tiny by comparison. "These are what you're after. Pale, barely green at all. Best, in fact, if they're still uncurling."

Piper remembered the spell:

Boil three score of young, fresh leaves . . .

"I think you're right." She felt herself relax a bit. "Yes, I'll need the young leaves."

Emily nodded. "Thought so."

Piper counted the pale leaves. Emily knew what she was doing. The plants on the cart would yield at least twenty of the youngest leaves for each of the three herbs.

"Yes," Piper said, "I'll take those." She waited, uncertain. "So, I just get them home, snip off the smallest leaves . . ."

Emily looked at her, frowning. "You don't want to discuss your business, and I respect that." She paused, seeming to look for a way to go on. "But I don't think you want to be snipping anything just yet."

"I need to—" Piper stopped herself. "I need those leaves in a hurry."

"I have no doubt. But you said you wanted to *plant* a garden. . . ." Emily watched Piper, waiting.

Piper thought back, reciting the spell again in her mind:

Plant a garden filled with these . . .

"You're right—again." Piper felt bad. "I'm sorry to be so secretive. Thank you, you're being very helpful." She smiled, trying again: "How do I best plant this garden if I want to harvest leaves quickly?"

"Now there's a question." Emily moved to a large, bare place in the dark, pungent earth. She picked up a stick and began to draw a pentagram. "I assume you know what this is," she said. Piper nodded, and Emily went on. "Set the top to the north. Plant one of your herbs at each of the five outer points." She pushed small holes with her stick into the five points, for emphasis. "It won't matter which herb you plant where, as they all go into your . . . your tea, or whatever you wish to brew."

Piper nodded, watching Emily intently.

"Now, you'll have more than a dozen plants total. So in each place where the lines that form the pentagram cross"—she pointed these out with her stick—"plant another herb." She drew a circle around the pentagram. "Any plants that you have left over, plant in this circle. Keep them within the circle, but not within the pentagram itself."

Piper nodded. "Got it."

"You may use any of the young leaves, but those from the plants at the five points of the pentagram will be the most powerful."

Piper looked at Emily. "I'll remember that."

"Prepare the ground before sundown, but plant by tonight's moon," said Emily. "If you know any—any words to help plants grow, say them then."

"I know a spell for that," said Piper, loosening her desire to try to keep secrets from this woman.

"Good. Tomorrow morning, wait for the dew to dry, then pick your leaves soon after, before the heat of the sun begins to affect them."

"Thank you."

"Do you need anything else? A nice fern for your bathroom, perhaps?"

"No," said Piper, "just these."

Emily nodded and began to wheel the cart back into the shop.

Piper walked along beside her. "Thanks for your advice. My Grams knew all that kind of stuff, but she died before she could teach me a lot of it."

"What was her name?" Emily asked. "Perhaps I knew her."

"Penny."

Emily stopped. "Penny Halliwell?"

Piper nodded.

Emily considered something, then began to push the cart again. "I remember Penny. She came in often. She was a wonderful woman."

"Yes," said Piper, smiling. "She was."

When they got to the counter, Emily looked at the herbs, seeming to add in her head. Piper noticed that there wasn't a cash register on the counter, or anywhere that she could see.

Emily looked up. "Thirty-eight dollars even."

Piper fished out the money and handed it to her.

Emily took it, then placed her hand over Piper's. "You are brewing a calming potion, and from the amount of herbs you're using, you need it for something powerful. Perhaps even something evil."

Piper watched her, unsure of what, if anything, to say.

"You wish to keep your business to yourself. So did your grandmother. But know this." She leaned in closer, speaking lower. "The power of the herbs you're brewing—the power of that spell you don't wish to speak of—will be greatly affected by how closely you follow the planting and harvesting information."

"I understand."

"I have no doubt that you are a powerful witch, as was your grandmother before you. But be careful. The slightest misstep may render your potion too weak to do what you need it to do."

"Thank you," said Piper. "Again."

Emily nodded. "Take the cart out to your car. You can leave it by the door."

Piper took the handle of the cart, then turned back. "I hope to see you again sometime."

Emily nodded. "Blessed be," she said, and walked through to the back room.

Chapter Fourteen

Paige and Phoebe walked into the Manor. "Let's check in with Piper," Paige said, "and then I want to take a shower. I still smell like that Dumpster."

"And whose fault is that?" Phoebe looked around for Piper. "Hello?"

Leo walked into the living room, holding Wyatt. "If you're looking for Piper, she's in the back."

Paige gave him a funny look. "The back . . . yard?"

Leo nodded. "She's getting ready to plant a garden."

Paige and Phoebe walked though the house and out to the yard.

Piper was working in a pair of overalls, wearing a large, straw sun hat. Gloves covered her hands as she shoveled out a wide circle in the backyard. The sod she'd cut out of the circle was stacked neatly on a flattened cardboard box. A small radio, tuned to a news station, sat on the sod.

"So," Paige said, watching her, "we're out increasing the demon population and you're . . . what . . . replacing the grass?"

"Planting those herbs," Piper said. She pointed to the plants she'd bought, now sitting in the shade of a tree. "They're for a spell that might get the demon to calm down."

"Oh?" Paige looked doubtful. "And a calmer version will . . . run amok slower?"

"A calmer version," said Piper, still working, "will sleep for a while, giving us time to figure out how to get it back into the egg before it lays waste to San Francisco."

"That laying-waste part may already be starting," said Phoebe.

She and Paige filled Piper in on their adventure with the armored truck.

"Thirteen," Piper repeated. She thought for a minute. "What about this Captain Rodgers guy? Do you think he's going to substantially increase the demon population?"

"Darryl's going to talk to him," said Paige. "Although it'll be a tough sell to convince the captain not to escalate. He watched eight demons climb out of that truck and run away."

"That wasn't on the news," Piper said.

"No," Phoebe agreed. "Somehow, Darryl kept the press away. But he can't keep doing it for long."

"One press helicopter over that scene today and it would be all over TV right now," said Paige.

"All the more reason to finish this garden." Piper looked back at the circle. "Is there any of Grams's compost left?"

"It should *all* be left," said Phoebe, "since we've never used it."

Piper glanced at the small wooden container in the corner of the yard. "How long does compost last, anyway?"

"It's compost," said Paige. "How can it go bad?"

"It's just—" Piper stopped. "This has to be a powerful potion. And for it to work at its best, the herbs have to be at their best." She looked at the dirt of the circle she'd cut from the lawn. "I want the earth we plant them in to smell and look like the earth at the Enchanted Garden."

"Grams's compost should do it," said Phoebe. "Remember how she'd carry all the fruit and veggie scraps down there? Then she'd say that poem."

Piper nodded. "I do remember. That 'poem' was a blessing. That's why we're going to use this compost. It's been imbued with Grams's powers. Then we're going to recite that blessing again."

The three walked to the compost bin, in the shade of a tree in the corner of the property. Piper pulled the lid off, reached in, and scooped out a handful. She lifted the compost to her nose, taking a deep whiff.

Paige crinkled her own nose as she watched her. "What are you doing?"

Piper held the compost out to Paige. "What does this smell like to you?"

Paige stepped back, but Phoebe moved in closer, taking a cautious sniff. She smiled. "It smells like . . ." She tried to pin it down. "Like the forest, when we used to go camping."

"Yes," said Piper. "That's what I was trying to remember. The Enchanted Garden smells like this too—like the forest when you walk in it." She crossed back to the circle, retrieved her shovel, and returned to the compost bin, using the shovel to fill Grams's old bucket, which still sat beside the bin. "We should have kept this going," she said, gesturing toward the compost bin. "It never occurred to me that Grams wasn't doing this just for the environment. There are spells that need herbs. Herbs that we can grow." She handed the bucket to Paige. "Spread this over the circle and then bring it back."

Paige looked doubtful, then sighed. "Might as well. I was going to take a shower anyway."

When they'd covered the circle in the lawn with a layer of compost, Piper began to work it into the soil with the shovel. Phoebe knelt down next to her and started turning the compost over with a hand trowel.

"Gee," said Paige, "too bad we don't have any more tools."

Piper pointed at the rake leaning against the back of the house. "Go get that," she said, "and you can even out what Phoebe and I turn over."

In a few minutes the circle was a smooth, dark patch of sweet-smelling earth.

"That's what I wanted," said Piper, satisfied. She looked at her sisters. "Thanks."

"Yeah," said Paige, trying to brush the damp earth from her hands, "let's do that again soon."

"So," said Phoebe, looking over at the herbs sitting in the shade, "now we plant?"

"Nope," said Piper, "now we wait for the moon."

"I'm first for the shower," said Paige, dropping the rake and heading toward the house.

Piper called after her: "Paige? One more thing?"

Paige came back, shielding her eyes from the sun.

"I think if we recite the blessing together, it'll be stronger."

The look in Paige's eye softened. "Sure," she said, "the Power of Three." She took Piper's hand, then Phoebe's. "But you two will have to teach it to me. I never got to hear Grams say any poem over the garbage."

Piper thought for a moment. "As I recall, it was kind of long."

"Now that you mention it," said Phoebe, "it

did seem longer than the other little poems she taught us."

"But it was catchy." Piper closed her eyes and began:

> *From earth you sprang, and grew, and bloomed,*
> *Till plucked from farmer's field.*
> *We brought you home, you fed us well,*
> *But you have more to yield.*

Phoebe joined her and the two sisters recited together:

> *The minerals you sucked from stone,*
> *The sun you drank from sky,*
> *Are stored within your roots and leaves*
> *To grow now, by and by.*
> *So rest here, till you decompose*
> *And then start life anew*
> *As flow'r, or tree, or herb or such,*
> *A-sparkling with the dew.*

"That's it?" asked Paige. "I can remember that much. Do it again."

"No," said Piper, "that's not all. There's more." She and Phoebe started again.

> *The miracle of life*
> *Is that it circles, round and round.*
> *You are not gone merely because*

You've turned up in the ground.
So rise again, fair stuff of life,
Become the grass, or wood.
You aid us best that grow'th best,
Now once more, do some good.

Piper stared at the compost. "When we were little, I thought this was just one more thing that Grams did differently from my friends' families. But as I got older, I realized that this is more than a simple incantation thanking the food we ate for growing."

Phoebe nodded. "That part at the end, about doing good, that was Grams preparing this compost for an herb garden, for some way to put more good into the world." She looked at Piper. "Just like you are now."

Piper nodded. "I think you're right." She looked at Paige. "Do you think you could recite that?"

"Really? It *is* long." Paige looked at her sisters. "Go slow, and I think I can follow along."

The three recited Grams's incantation over the circle of earth. When they'd finished, they were quiet for a moment.

Paige broke the spell. "I see now. This is more than some old dirt. This is, like, recycling charmed stuff."

"Yeah," said Piper.

Paige looked at her hands, rubbing the fine, dark earth that stained her fingers. "So, this dirt has its own magic." She looked up. "But I still want to be first in the shower." Without waiting for a response, she turned and went back into the house.

After dinner, the three sisters sat in the living room. The television was on, tuned to a local channel that would switch to any late-breaking news, but the volume was low. No reports of any mayhem appeared.

"This doesn't feel right," said Paige. "He's out there, all thirteen versions of him, and we're sitting in here, waiting for him to strike."

"No," Piper reminded her. "We're waiting for the moon to rise—at least, I am."

Phoebe stood. "Do you need help planting the garden?"

"I don't think so," said Piper. "You two were a big help today in preparing the soil and blessing the spot, but I think I'm good now."

Phoebe looked at Paige. "Then maybe you and I should do the Batman-and-Robin thing and go cruising Gotham looking for trouble."

"Good idea," said Paige. "But no tights, okay? Not a good look for me." She crossed to the stairs. "Let me check on Chase real quick, then we can go fight crime."

Paige walked into the attic, crossed to the cot, and sat. Chase opened his eyes, watching her. "Hey," she said softly. "Just wanted to check in with you. You hungry?"

He blinked once.

"Thirsty?"

Again, he blinked once.

"You're good, then?"

He blinked twice.

Paige was beginning to think that she could read whole expressions in Chase's eyes. Today, those eyes seemed depressed. She rubbed his arm lightly. "I'll bet that this is *really* starting to get old."

After a moment, he blinked twice.

"Thought so." She leaned a little closer. "This must be such a bummer for you. But here's the good news: You're safe, you're alive, and you're with the very people who can help you get back to normal."

He blinked twice. She almost thought she could see him nod in resigned agreement.

"I wish there were a way to make this right for you today," she said, "and make you all better right now." She shook her head. "All I can say is that we're doing the best we can."

He blinked twice, this time with no hesitation.

"Good." She patted his arm again. "We're going out again tonight to try to stop this guy. One of these days, we'll get him."

He blinked twice again.

She rose, bent over, and kissed him softly on the lips. "Hang in there," she said. "This will all be over soon, I promise."

She turned before she could see the response in his eyes.

Phoebe looked up as Paige came down the stairs. They linked arms when Paige reached the bottom, and turned back to Piper. "We're off to do good," Phoebe said in a mock-serious tone.

Piper smiled faintly as they walked out the front door. She listened to the sound of the car driving away, then sighed at the sudden quiet. She checked the eastern sky for signs of moonlight. Seeing none, she went into Wyatt's room.

Leo sat in the rocking chair, holding Wyatt. "He just fell asleep," he said softly. He stood up and turned, about to put Wyatt into his crib.

"Wait," said Piper. "Give him to me."

"But he's—"

"I know. Asleep." She held out her arms. "I just want to hold him for a while."

Leo carefully transferred the bundled baby to Piper. She sat in the rocker, putting it gently in motion. She rearranged the blanket, which was wrapped up around Wyatt's face, then brushed his fine, downy hair with her finger.

"He's so tiny," she said softly. "He's a good reminder of why we need to put that demon back where he came from."

"Just him?" Leo's eyes twinkled a bit. "What about the rest of San Francisco?"

Piper looked up at him wearily. "I can't hold the rest of San Francisco in my arms."

"Ah. You're looking to recharge."

"I'm *looking*," Piper began, sounding just a tad irritated, "to spend five quiet minutes with my son." She sighed. "Just five minutes. Then I'll go back to saving the rest of San Francisco."

"You got it," said Leo. He rose and left the room quietly.

Piper closed her eyes and began to hum a soft lullaby. She rocked and hummed, held her baby, and for a few minutes forgot about demons. Wyatt, still fast asleep, wrapped his hand around her little finger. She smiled, then looked out of the window.

The quarter moon, with its faint outline completing the circle, was rising, cresting the tops of the trees in the backyard, tipping their leaves with silver. Piper looked back down at Wyatt. "Even when you're sleeping," she said, "you're looking out for me."

She rose, kissed him, and placed him gently into his crib.

Piper stood in the backyard, waiting for her eyes to adjust to the moonlight. She offered a blessing to the four horizons, then oriented herself to the north. She turned the shovel over in her hands and with the tip of the handle began to draw a pentagram on the circle of fresh-turned earth. When she'd finished that, she took a bulb planter and punched a hole at each of the five points, and at the five places where the pentagram's lines intersected. Finishing this, she drew a circle around the outside of the pentagram and punched a few more holes inside the circle. These holes were to be her markers.

She put the herbs into Grams's wheelbarrow, moved them close to the circle, and lifted the first one out, taking her time, deciding where it should be placed. She knelt, widened one of the holes with her trowel, then carefully removed the plant from its pot, lowered it into the hole, and tucked its roots in, patting the enriched soil around the stalk until she was satisfied that it was well supported and straight. She went on to the next one, then the next, moving around the pentagram in a clockwise circle.

The moon was nearly overhead as she tamped the last of the herbs into place.

"Piper?"

She turned to see Leo in the semidarkness. "Hey."

"Are you having any trouble? Do you need some help?"

"No. I'm fine. Why?"

"You've been out here for nearly three hours."

"Really? Wow." Piper patted down the last bit of earth and stood up. "Well, I'm finished now."

Leo surveyed her work. "Cool garden."

"Yeah," said Piper. "Maybe we'll keep it."

"You should come get some sleep," said Leo. "You have to be up at dawn, right?"

"Right," said Piper. "I almost forgot that part."

She stood next to Leo, wrapping her arm around his waist. "What's a good blessing for plants?"

"You're asking me?"

"We recited Grams's blessing for the compost earlier," she told him. "I was just thinking we ought to bless the plants, too, now that they're in the garden."

"You're the witch. Make something up."

Piper frowned at him, then got into the spirit of the moment. She raised her hands, spreading them out, and closed her eyes.

Herbs within this garden patch,
Drink deep of nature's food.
Rise up, grow strong; before too long,
We both shall do some good.

"Not bad," said Leo. "Did you really just make that up?"

"Yep."

"I like the way it ties you and the herbs together."

She turned, still holding him around his waist, and they headed back toward the house. "I don't know if I like that part all *that* well, but it's true, whether I like it or not."

Leo stopped walking. He turned as if he

heard something, but Piper could tell from the look on his face that what he was listening to was internal. "What is it?" she asked.

"It's your sisters," he said. "They're in trouble."

Chapter Fifteen

The flames rose toward the moon, causing it to shimmer and ripple in the waves generated by the heat. Phoebe lay on the sidewalk, trying to get her bearings and remember where she was. She looked around.

A line of flaming debris spread down the street for nearly half a block. Flames towered out of the warehouse, reaching into the night sky.

"Man," muttered Phoebe, "this demon is really into explosions." She rose up on one elbow, realizing that she hurt in a dozen places, and focused on the shapes moving in and out of the shadows a short distance away. Demons. Phoebe tried to count, but her vision still blurred.

As she watched, one demon carried what appeared to be a gruesome bundle of body parts to the street, where he dumped them unceremoniously. The parts began to reform, metamorphosing into two.

"Fourteen," Phoebe whispered. She turned, seeing the same thing happening a short distance away. "Fifteen . . ." She glanced down the street. "Sixteen."

She tried to rise further, then winced, turning to Paige. "Let's get out of here," she said. "This Batman-and-Robin thing isn't working."

There was no answer.

Phoebe crawled closer to where Paige lay, unmoving. "Paige? Honey, you've got to get up. We have to get out of here."

Paige's face looked pale, eerily lit by the flickering flames, causing it to go in and out of shadow, but Phoebe saw no movement in her face; not even the flutter of an eyelash.

"Please, Paige," Phoebe whispered, "you're too big to carry, and I'm too banged up even if you weren't."

The shadows stopped flickering, becoming solid across Paige's face. Phoebe realized that something—or someone—was blocking the light.

She looked up. A demon stood before her, holding a long, heavy sword. His shirt was nearly torn in two, and one button fell to the sidewalk in front of her. As Phoebe watched, his singed, blackened face began to heal itself until it looked like Chase's once again. The clothes remained in tatters.

"Seventeen." Phoebe picked up the button, then gently prodded Paige with one hand while trying to engage the demon in conversation. "You guys blew this warehouse up just to get some swords that you like?"

The demon nodded, a half smile on his lips.

"What's so special about these swords?"

The demon raised the sword shoulder high, slashed it viciously through the air, then made a line with one finger across his throat.

"Oh," said Phoebe, "beheadings."

The demon nodded. He stepped closer. "Thank . . . you," he said. He began to draw the sword back, seeming to measure the distance to Phoebe's head.

The sound of a car hurtling toward them caught both their attentions. The demon looked over his shoulder to see Piper's car racing down the street straight at him. She slammed hard into the demon, hurtling him twenty feet into the air as the car skidded to a stop.

Piper jumped out of the car, crossing to Phoebe as Leo orbed next to Paige, disappearing with her. Piper helped Phoebe into the car, then climbed into the driver's seat and closed the door. The demon in front of them rose, on its way to becoming two.

"Eighteen," said Phoebe. She looked behind her. "Piper, they're all coming after us."

Piper floored the car and backed into the demons, hitting several and sending them flying. She changed gears and sped down the street.

"That didn't do any good," said Phoebe. "You already killed one with your car."

"I know," said Piper, "but it sure *felt* good." She looked over at Phoebe. "You look awful," she said. "What happened?"

"Paige got a sense of where they were strongest, and we followed it," said Phoebe. "We got down here, saw them breaking into that warehouse." She touched her arm gingerly, making sure it wasn't broken. "The funny thing was, they didn't seem to be out only for mayhem this time. It looked more like a simple robbery." She ran a finger under a rip in her jeans, examining the gash in her thigh there. "We decided that there was only one Innocent in danger, and that was the guard, and he was sleeping. So just when we thought that this was merely a burglary, the guard woke up, hit some alarm, and took off running down the street. Before I could even wonder why, boom. The whole place goes up. And I wake up on the street, next to Paige." She looked at Piper. "How did you find us?"

"Leo," said Piper. "I told him to stay with Wyatt and Chase, but just as I got here, he orbed in and got Paige out. I guess he knew I'd need the help."

"Good thing," said Phoebe. "That last demon was about to show me what they want to do with their new toys."

"What do they want to do?"

"Behead people."

Piper nodded. "That makes sense, in its own, sick way."

"Yeah. Not even Darryl will be able to keep a string of beheadings out of the news."

"Plus, if they're done by an unstoppable small army of look-alikes—"

"The panic will set in," said Phoebe, finishing the thought. "And our own army won't be far behind."

Piper looked at the horizon. "It'll be dawn in a few hours," she said. "As soon as the dew dries on my herbs, I'm making that potion."

"And then what?"

"And then . . ." Piper trailed off. "I'm not sure. Then we find a way to get them all back into that egg. But at least, if that potion works, they won't be running around beheading people."

Phoebe limped into the house, holding on to Piper.

"Leo?" Piper called out.

"I'm in the attic with Paige."

"You go up," said Phoebe. "I think I'll just lie down here and moan for a while."

"Nope. Sorry. You need to be healed too."

Phoebe looked at the stairs and groaned.

"Come on," said Piper. "We'll take them one at a time."

Phoebe began to limp slowly up the stairs, still leaning heavily on Piper.

They hobbled into the attic together, expecting

to see Leo and Paige chatting softly about what had happened. Instead, Paige lay on the floor. Leo was leaning over her, still in the midst of his healing.

Leo looked drained. Paige was still unconscious.

Piper let go of Phoebe and stepped forward. "Honey? What is it?"

Leo looked up. "Apparently, even though her injuries and Phoebe's were precipitated by something evil—the explosion—the blast itself, and the injuries caused by their *landing* from the blast, are from the mortal realm."

"Does that mean you can't heal her?"

"I'm not sure." He rose, crossed to Phoebe, and held his hand over the gash in her thigh. His hand glowed. The wound visibly improved, but did not completely heal. He stepped back a bit. "How does that feel?"

Phoebe tested the leg, attempting to walk on it. "Hey," she said. "Quite a bit better."

"But not all the way better?" Leo watched her.

"No," she admitted. "I guess not."

Leo nodded solemnly, turning to Piper. "Paige's injuries are to her head, probably caused by landing on the sidewalk after being blown out of the warehouse. And since the blast itself wasn't supernatural . . ."

Piper nodded. "I get it. No demon shot her out of the building with his power."

"That guard," Phoebe remembered, "he knew

something was up. He took off running before the explosion."

"And he was mortal," said Leo.

"But you are helping her, right?" Piper looked over to where Paige lay. "She is going to be all right, isn't she?"

"I'm not sure." Leo, too, looked over at Paige. "I've done all I can for her. I think she should be seen by a doctor."

Phoebe nodded. "If she has a concussion—or worse, if she's got a blood clot on her brain or something . . ."

Piper understood. "You two have to take her to the doctor." She looked at her watch. "It's late. Maybe the emergency room won't be that busy. With any luck, a doctor can treat her right away. And he can look at your injuries too, Phoebes." She shooed them toward Paige. "Go. Now. Time might be really important. I'll stay with Chase and Wyatt."

"Get some sleep," Leo said. "You have to be picking herbs as soon as the dew dries."

Piper nodded. "I'll be fine. You make sure Paige gets looked after."

Leo lifted Paige into his arms. He turned to Phoebe. "Can you make the stairs on your own?"

"Sure," she said. "I really am a lot better."

"Good," said Leo. "Let's go." He walked out of the attic, Phoebe following behind.

Piper sighed. She kneeled down and checked

on Chase, who watched her closely with his eyes. She patted his arm. "What a world, huh?" She rose. "Get some sleep. I'm sure Paige is going to be fine."

She walked out, wishing she'd meant what she'd just said.

Chapter Sixteen

Piper stood in the kitchen, laying out her mortar and pestle and other potion-making tools, when she heard the car in the driveway. She met Leo at the door. He had Paige in his arms. "Where's Phoebe?" Piper asked.

"I dropped her off at the warehouse so she could pick up the other car," Leo said. She's right behind me."

They climbed to the attic, where Leo laid Paige down on a cot next to Chase's, making her comfortable. "What are you doing?" Piper asked. "Why not put her in her own room?"

"She insisted on being up here," Leo said. "Where she can keep an eye on Chase."

Phoebe walked in as Piper looked Paige over carefully. "So she's all right? She came to?"

"She did, for a while," said Phoebe. "They think she's going to be fine. At least, she should be."

"What does that mean, exactly?"

Leo finished tucking a blanket around Paige and rose, crossing to Piper. "It's a concussion," he said. "The good news is that there's no sign of bleeding, no apparent damage to the brain."

Piper watched him warily. "What's the bad news?"

"While she sleeps, she could slip into unconsciousness again. So someone needs to wake her every two hours."

Piper rubbed her own head. "Why was she unconscious for so long?"

"They couldn't find a reason for it at the hospital," said Leo.

"Could it be because it was something demonic behind the something mortal that knocked her out?" Piper asked.

"Maybe." Leo touched Piper lightly on the shoulder. "That's why she's better off here, with the three of us to watch her. I'll start. You two get some rest. Tomorrow could be a really big day."

"Right." Piper kissed Leo lightly. "Be sure to wake me before the sun's all the way up."

Leo nodded. Piper and Phoebe headed toward the living room.

"How's your leg?" asked Piper, watching the way Phoebe descended the stairs.

"Sore." Phoebe walked down a few more steps, as if testing her leg's health. "But getting better."

"An injury like that would normally have

required several stitches, and taken weeks to completely heal."

Phoebe nodded. "Yeah. That's why I think Paige is going to be better soon."

Piper looked out the window at the eastern sky, lighter already, with the faintest touch of pink above the skyline. "It's almost dawn," she said. "Let's get some rest."

Leo gently shook Piper's shoulder to wake her. She sat up, looking out the window. Light softly flooded the room, but she could tell that the sun hadn't yet risen.

"How's Paige?" she asked.

"About the same."

Piper nodded. "Phoebe's watching her?"

"Yeah."

She got out of bed, stretched, and ran a hand through her hair. "Do you think I have time to take a shower before I—"

Before she could finish the sentence, Leo wrapped her in an embrace and held her.

Piper relaxed into it, almost to the point of letting herself sag into his arms. For one moment, she forgot everything and simply enjoyed being held.

She took a deep breath, let it out, and placed her hands gently on his shoulders, stepping back a bit. "Thanks. I needed that."

"Thought so."

"How do we stop him, Leo? Even if I slow

him down, how, without Paige, without the Power of Three—"

"Shhhh . . . don't think like that. Otherwise, I'm going to have to hug you again."

She smiled. "Right. One thing at a time. Let's see if I can stop the mayhem, then we'll figure out where to go from there."

Piper slipped into her robe and walked out to check the herb garden. Just outside the door she stopped, struck by its simple beauty: a dozen or so plants with long green leaves, arranged in a pattern on the dark, musty earth they'd worked the day before. Every plant glistened with dew, which formed translucent pearls on the leaves.

She took a breath, feeling the damp grass under her feet. The birds sang, the trees reached up into the pale sky, the garden smelled like Grams's. There was still peace in the world, she thought, and she and her sisters would find a way to keep it there.

She turned, went back into the house, and climbed the stairs to the attic.

"How is she?" Piper asked as she walked in.

"She's still a little groggy when I wake her." Phoebe stroked Paige's forehead gently. "And in her sleep she mumbles a little, like she's dreaming."

"Let's hope she's all the way back with us soon." Piper smiled at Chase, who was watching her closely. "'Morning," she said. "We'll have you both fixed up before long." She knelt next to Phoebe. "After I get myself cleaned up I'm taking my breakfast out to the yard with me. As soon as I see the last dewdrop dry off the herbs . . ."

"Got it," Phoebe said.

"We're going to be okay. We're going to beat this thing."

"Glad to hear it."

Piper rose and walked out of the attic.

Showered, dressed, and munching on the last of her bagel, Piper watched the sun filter across the yard and felt the grass dry under her feet. She knelt down to check on the progress of the plants. The leaves of the herbs were dry, but some of the stalks still seemed damp. Just when she decided that shouldn't matter, the stalks, too, dried, almost as if by magic.

Piper rose, opened the first of three small bags she'd brought with her, and stepped into the garden. She worked on the plants at the points of the pentagram first, beginning with the mugwort. She carefully pinched the youngest leaves at their stems, placing them into the bag, counting as she went. She moved on to the moonwort plants, stopping now and then to consider whether a small leaf from an inner plant or a slightly larger one from an outer plant would work best. The sun crept full force into the yard. She picked up her pace, turning to the madwort, growing more confident in her ability to choose the best leaves as she went.

When each bag held exactly twenty leaves, she went into the kitchen and began to prepare the potion.

Leo walked in and leaned over the simmering kettle on the stove. "Wow, that smells . . . good. Different, but good."

"It's almost simmered long enough," said Piper, looking at her timer.

"You're making a tea?"

"Yeah. We want the strongest sleeping-pill effect," she said. "So I think the full-strength tea is the way to go."

"How long will it stay potent?"

"Three days. But I don't want to mess around. I want him to drink it today. This morning, if we can manage it."

The timer went off. Piper strained the contents of the kettle through a mesh and into a small earthen crock, then sealed the crock with a rubber-lined lid. "Now," she said, "let's say you're a demon from ancient Greece. How, and when, and where do you decide you're thirsty for some nice tea?"

"Do you know any spells to make him want to drink it?"

Piper stopped a moment, considering. "We can't kill him, we can't banish him, and the spells we *have* tried on him have only made things worse, so I hadn't thought of that. But maybe we can induce him to be thirsty for what's in this crock." She smiled, gave Leo a peck on the cheek, and hurried up to the attic.

"What's up?" Phoebe asked as Piper came into the room.

"I need a spell to make that demon want to drink my tea," said Piper, moving to the Book of Shadows. "Know any, offhand?"

"No," said Phoebe. "I don't remember ever seeing a spell like that."

"Neither do I," said Piper. "But I wish I did. We need to hurry, while the potion is at its strongest."

"Mulumor," mumbled Paige.

Piper looked over to where Paige lay, her eyes still closed. "Was that an answer?"

"Maybe," said Phoebe. "Last time I woke her up, she was pretty normal. But after she went back to sleep, she kept trying to talk, except that her answers didn't make any sense." She brushed Paige's forehead. "Isn't that right, Paige?"

"Murphr, n thnkit."

Piper turned back to the Book. "Let's let her sleep. That's what she needs most. Right now I have to find this spell."

"Look . . . up . . . 'murmurlr' . . . ," said Paige.

Piper turned, staring at Paige. She walked from the Book to the cot where Paige lay. "What did you say, hon?"

Paige's eyes stayed closed, but her mouth moved, forming words. "The spell . . . you want . . . murmurlr."

Phoebe leaned closer. "Sweetie, we can't understand you."

Paige frowned. "The spell . . . to drink . . ."

"Yes," said Piper. "A spell to make him drink."

Paige nodded ever so slightly. "Um-hmm . . ."

Phoebe looked at Piper. "She can hear us. She's trying to tell you something."

"Look . . . under . . ." Paige drifted off.

"Paige?"

This time, there was no answer.

Piper looked at Phoebe. "'Mullamur.' What does that sound like to you?"

"I don't think she said 'mullamur,'" said Phoebe. "It sounded more like 'mulumor.'"

"'Mull'? As in 'mulled'?" Piper thought for a moment. "That makes some sort of sense. It's a drink. But my potion isn't mulled. Hot, but not mulled."

Paige mumbled again.

Piper leaned closer. "Paige? Do you know a spell?"

Paige frowned. "Mullamor . . ."

Piper looked at Phoebe. "'Mull *amour*'? As in, to mull over love? Is she talking about a potion to make the drinker think about love?"

Phoebe patted Paige's hand. "Nice try, but I don't think making the demon bring us flowers and candy is going to solve our problems."

"Phoebe," Piper began, "there are no spells in the Book to make men bring us gifts to show their love. I don't think that's what she's saying." She stopped. "But there is a spell to reduce a man's pride."

"Um-hmmm . . . ," said Paige.

"That's it," said Phoebe, "that's what she's trying to tell us."

"Mull, to think over. *'Amour-propre,'*—excessive pride," Piper paused. "Didn't Paige use a spell like that once?"

"Yeah," said Phoebe, "but it backfired, since Paige wanted that guy to be less prideful for selfish reasons."

"Still, there must be something in that spell, something she remembers, something she wants us to know."

"Um-hmmm . . . ," said Paige. Her eyes were still closed, but she nodded her head more fully this time.

Piper moved to the Book, flipping through its pages. "Here it is," she said, "a potion to reduce a man's pride." She read further. "And, since a man that prideful isn't likely to want to drink what you offer him"—she looked up at Phoebe, smiling—"here's a charm to make him *want* to drink the potion."

"Yes . . . ," said Paige softly.

Piper read the charm listed in the Book.

● ● ●

When the plume of pride consumes a man
But he'll not take your offer,
Blow him kisses, soft and sweet
Before you make your proffer.
Then whisper these words on the air
That blows in his direction,
'Drink the drink I give to you.'
He'll bow to your suggestion.

"That sounds almost too easy," said Piper. She crossed to the cots, kneeling beside Paige. "Thanks." She patted her hand. "You get better. We'll need you at full strength soon, I'm afraid."

"Full . . . strnnnn . . . ," mumbled Paige.

Piper stood, turning to Phoebe. "I want to take Leo with me so we can find the head demon and orb right to him. Can you watch Wyatt and Chase *and* Paige?"

"No sweat," said Phoebe. "I'll hold down the fort. You go deliver the knockout punch."

"Punch," said Piper. "Very clever."

Chapter Seventeen

Piper filled Leo in on her plan. He looked less than thrilled.

"So," he said, "you want to find the original demon, walk up to him, hand him the crock, walk away, determine which way the wind is blowing, say your charm, and wait for him to drink the potion?"

"It does sound a little harder when you put it that way." Piper thought a moment. "Let's track him down. Maybe, when we find him, something will come to me."

Together, they scried for the demons, using the button that had fallen off the shirt of one of them.

"This is the strongest reading," said Leo. "He's in the financial district again, near the Transamerica Pyramid building."

Piper picked up the crock of tea and took Leo's hand. "Let's go."

They appeared in the small, narrow Red-wood Park alongside the towering Transamerica Pyramid. Piper stopped, touching the redwood tree they'd orbed in next to. "It's so peaceful here," she said. "Such a nice oasis in the middle of all the skyscrapers."

"Maybe that's a good thing," said Leo. "After all, you *are* looking to lull this demon."

"Yeah," said Piper. "Let's hope this is a good sign."

Leo looked around them. "Over there," he said.

The demon sat on a bench under one of the trees, watching the base of the pyramid.

Piper took a step closer to him. "I hope we're not too late to stop whatever destruction he has planned next."

"We can't worry about that right now," said Leo. "Right now, we have to figure out how to get him to drink from that crock."

"I have an idea," said Piper. "Stick close, and if you need to, orb us out of here."

"Piper, what—"

Before he could finish, Piper was walking confidently toward the demon. Leo hurried to catch up.

The Chase look-alike stared up at her suspiciously.

"Hello," said Piper. She sat on a bench not far from the demon. The hilt of his beheading sword peeked out from a long duffel bag at his feet.

The demon eyed her, but said nothing. He glanced to Leo, who sat within an easy arm's reach of Piper.

"I've brought you something," she said, placing the crock on the bench between them.

"If you wish to poison me," said the demon, "then I will, again, have need to thank you."

"It isn't poison," Piper said, "it's a peace offering."

The demon laughed. "I am not a creature of peace. I am not a creature of kindness or understanding. I am fear. Terror. Rage. Destruction. I am here to end the world as you know it, to bring about another millennium of darkness."

"If you are too proud to accept my gift," said Piper, "then I humbly withdraw."

She put her finger into her mouth, then held it up. She glanced back to Leo. "Come. This way."

They both rose, Leo keeping a careful eye on the demon. They walked upwind of him twenty feet or so.

"That was pretty clever," said Leo.

"The spell is designed to combat pride. I thought I should get that in somehow." Piper watched the demon, who was still eyeing them suspiciously. "Here goes," she said. She leaned toward him, blew a kiss, and said:

Drink the drink I give to you.

They waited. For a moment, nothing happened. The demon still stared at them. "Let's move farther back," she said, "and give it a chance to work."

They walked as far back in the mini-park as they could, along the narrow strip of redwood trees that ran down one side of the building, past the open-air tables, to the frog fountain. Here, they sat in the shade, next to the geysers of water that rose up in the center of the circle of frogs, the frogs themselves all small statues on green metal lily pads.

Leo pulled Piper next to him and nuzzled her. "Look at me," he said. "Let's check him out from the corners of our eyes."

Piper looked up at him. "You got it," she said, wrapping her arms around him. She laid her head on his shoulder, glancing toward the demon again.

Nothing. The demon still stared them down.

"What if this only works on people?" Piper asked.

"He's taken on human form. He's taken on a host body. You should still be okay."

"But nothing's happening." She sighed. "All that work. Buying the herbs, composting the soil, laying out the garden . . ."

"Hold on," said Leo.

"Hey, I think I've got a right to whine if I want to."

"No. Not that. He's reaching for the crock."

Piper froze, daring to glance over Leo's shoulder.

The demon stretched both arms out for the pot slowly, tentatively, then pulled his arms back again. He looked at Piper and Leo.

"At the very least," said Leo, "he's curious."

Piper stole another glance. The demon picked up the crock this time, pulling it into his lap. He sniffed the top, then carefully undid the latch.

"He's not looking over here anymore," whispered Leo. "That smell's got him."

The demon bent his head, inhaling deeper, then brought the crock to his lips. He took a small sip, then sat back. He started to look over at Piper and Leo, then looked back at the crock, taking a bigger sip.

"He's hooked," Leo said.

The demon picked the crock up, tipped his head back, and took gulp after gulp of the nectar inside.

"That's it," said Leo. "He's finished it. Except for the bit he spilled down the front of his shirt." He took Piper's hand. "Let's go back and check on everybody at the Manor."

"Wait," she said. "He's still a powerful demon. Let's stick around for a little while longer."

The demon scratched his head and yawned. A birdcall in the tree above him caught his attention. He looked up, spotted the bird, and smiled. He leaned back on the bench and closed his eyes, a look of contentment spreading across his face.

Piper watched a moment more before breathing out a long, heavy sigh. "I think this is working." She pulled her cell phone out of her purse and dialed. "Darryl, hi. It's Piper. Listen, two things. First, can you get a squad to check out the Pyramid? I don't know, for a bomb, say?" She glanced at Leo. "It's just that we tracked one of the demons here, and he was watching the building, maybe waiting for something." She nodded. "Yeah. Just to be safe. That's what I'm thinking." She looked over at the demon, who now appeared to be dozing. "Here's the other thing. I've put a spell on the demon and lulled him to sleep." She kept watching the demon. "No, I don't think you should arrest him. I'm afraid that waking him up will cause the spell to wear off." She nodded as she listened to Darryl. "Yeah, that's what I'm thinking. If you can put a team together and keep him under surveillance, that will help us a lot. We're going to try to learn how to vanquish him while he's . . . you know . . . not so dangerous. Thanks."

She snapped the phone closed, turning to Leo. "Darryl says he'll be here in ten minutes. Let's stick around until then, just in case this spell wears off really, really fast on demons."

Phoebe sat in the attic between Chase and Paige. She had Wyatt on one knee and a jar of strained pears on the other. She fed bite after bite to Chase, tracing her fingers down his chin and throat after each bite to make him swallow. Wyatt chewed on a teething ring while she bounced him gently up and down.

"I thought you might like to meet Wyatt," she said to Chase. "Then I remembered that you two met at the park, that first day you saw Paige." She fed Chase another bite. "I'm not sure what he thinks about you eating all his pears."

Phoebe made a face at Wyatt, but she kept talking to Chase. "I'm sure there's so much about all of this that's freaking you out right now, but really, Paige and Piper and I are just three sisters with the same kinds of issues other sisters have: jobs, taking care of Wyatt here, dealing with boyfriends and a brother-in-law. . . ." She fed Chase another bite, smoothing his throat with her fingers. "Then there's that other part. The part where we work to keep darker things at bay."

He blinked twice.

"I guess what I'm trying to say is . . ."

"Hang in there," Paige mumbled.

Phoebe put the spoon down. "Paige? Honey? You with us again?"

Paige nodded. "I already gave him that speech."

Wyatt gurgled.

Paige opened her eyes and smiled at the baby. "Hey, little man. It's good to see you, too."

Phoebe reached for Paige's hand and squeezed it. "Boy, you had us worried," she said. "You've taken your own sweet time about completely coming around."

"Funny, I feel like I've been here all along. I remember hearing conversations, not wanting you to wake me up, trying to tell Piper about that spell. . . ."

"Hey, that worked out, so far. Piper called just before I brought Wyatt up here. Looks like the demon's in slumber land."

"For how long?"

Phoebe shook her head. "We don't know. The potion is potent for three days, but with a demon . . ."

Paige nodded. "With a demon, he could be up and around in a lot less time."

Phoebe glanced at Wyatt. "Is it okay that Chase eats your pears, big boy?"

Wyatt made a sound like a giggle.

Phoebe nodded. "Good." She looked at Paige. "Let me get him changed and down for a nap, and I'll be back." She rose.

"Before you go," said Paige, "bring me the Book? We've got to find a way to vanquish that demon without killing him, and we've got to do it soon."

Phoebe placed Wyatt in Paige's arms, walked across the attic to retrieve the Book of Shadows, then traded Wyatt for the Book. She put a Japanese folding screen between the two cots, then looked behind the screen at Chase. "Hope you don't mind," she said. "Witch stuff." She turned back to Paige. "You just lie here and read," she said. "No trying to get up yet."

"Yes, nurse," said Paige.

Phoebe left, helping Wyatt wave good-bye as she did.

Paige settled in, putting an extra pillow behind her head to make reading easier. "Don't worry, Chase," she said. "The screen is just to keep you from getting any more involved in . . . you know . . . stuff you'd be better off not knowing about." For a moment she waited for an answer, then realized that no answer would be coming. She turned her attention to the Book. "Now," she whispered, "how to return a demon without killing it." She began to turn the pages slowly, carefully.

Phoebe came into the living room in time to see Piper and Leo orb in. "Hey," she said. "Just put Wyatt down. How'd it go?"

"So far, so good," said Piper. "He's sleeping on a bench in Redwood Park, just like any other homeless guy, only he's better dressed. And better looking."

"We talked to Darryl before we came back," said Leo. "He's going to have an elite team take shifts and watch the demon. We don't want him disturbed, and if he does wake up, we want someone who won't panic and try to arrest him, or worse, try to shoot him."

"That all sounds good," said Phoebe. "Hey, guess what? Paige is all the way awake now."

"That's great," said Piper. "I was starting to worry. How's she doing?"

"She's up on her cot, looking over the Book, trying to find a way to get all the demon copies back in that egg."

"I'll go give her a hand," said Piper. "The sooner we can take advantage of his snooze time, the better for everybody."

In the attic, Paige lay on the cot, her fingers softly running back and forth over a spell. Her eyes were red. Deep, sorrowful creases etched across her forehead. Others creased the corners of her mouth, turning them down.

"Paige?" Piper crossed to her quickly, kneeling beside her. "What's wrong? You look awful. Maybe we should take you back to the hospital."

"No," Paige said.

Her voice was so soft, Piper could barely hear her. "What is it?" Piper asked. "What's wrong?"

"I found . . . this," said Paige, her voice still only a cracked whisper. Her lip trembled. "I found . . . a way . . . to . . ." She choked up. Tears filled her eyes, though none ran from their pools.

"Paige, honey, what is it?"

Paige pointed at the Book. Piper leaned over and read the spell Paige's finger indicated.

When demon leech o'ertakes a man
To use his body ill,

And nothing in your conjuring
Will break him to your will;
When countless others stand to fall
Lest demon be reined in,
Then you must count the greater good
'Longside the greater sin.
For one way sure to mark thee
That the demon still shall lie,
Is to look unto the demon's source—
The human host must die.

Piper's hand went to her mouth. She read the words again, shaking her head as she did. She glanced over to Paige, whose tears were falling now in tiny rivulets down her cheeks.

Piper took Paige's hand in hers, squeezing it. "Leo," she called softly.

Leo appeared beside her. He took one look at their faces. "What's wrong?"

"Can you take Chase—and the egg, I suppose—somewhere? Phoebe, Paige, and I need to talk."

"Somewhere . . . nice," Paige managed. "Somewhere . . . you think he'd really like to see."

Leo glanced from Piper to Paige. "Sure," he said. He stepped behind the screen.

"Let's you and me get out of here," Piper heard him say, but she couldn't see them.

There was a bright glow from behind the screen, and Leo, Chase, and the demon's egg were gone.

"The Book has seemed a lot of things to me," said Paige, wiping her eyes, "but before today it never seemed cruel."

Phoebe walked in, and Piper showed her the spell, waiting while she read it. She looked up. "This is awful."

Paige sat up, tossing the Book onto the cot beside her. "This is worse than awful. I refuse to believe that this is the only way to get rid of that demon."

"Whoa. Paige." Phoebe put a steadying hand on Paige's shoulder. "Are you sure you should be sitting up?"

"I am *not* going to lie here while this Book tells me that our only option is to let Chase be killed."

"All right," said Piper, trying to restore a sense of balance, "let's break this down. Yes, that last line is awful. But look at what comes before. This is, like, a last resort. Only when we think we can't win. Only when the greater good is in big trouble."

"Look around," said Paige angrily. "We already know that the greater good is in huge trouble."

Piper spoke carefully. "You're right. We know that unless we do something, all of San Francisco will be a smoking wasteland soon. Phoebe's seen it. And we can guess, based on this demon's personal history, that he won't stop with destroying this city alone. Last time he was out and about, he brought the entire Greek civilization to its knees for a thousand years."

"And this time around," added Phoebe, "the world has much better weapons. This time, we could fight this monster until we'd bombed ourselves all the way back to the Stone Age."

"Phoebe, I don't think you're helping," said Piper.

"I get what's at stake here," said Paige. "And as soon as I saw this spell, as soon as I read it, I knew it would work." She looked at Piper. "You did too. But that doesn't mean that it's the only thing that will work."

Phoebe knelt beside Paige. "No. Of course not."

"Besides, we can't kill an Innocent," Paige said. "No matter how much we say it's for the greater good."

"No," Piper agreed. "Of course we can't. But the police could. The SWAT team could. Captain Rodgers could."

"Anyone who's seen that demon run amok could," Phoebe added.

Paige rose, testing her balance, then pushed back the Japanese screen. She stared at Chase's empty cot. "Anyone who's seen that sweet face while it was blowing things up, or terrorizing people at the bank, or—"

"We get it," said Piper. "Lots of people will be happy to do that part for us."

Paige turned back to her sisters. "I'm not ready to give up."

"Okay," said Piper. "Let's make *sure* that there's no other way to do this."

"Well, let's make sure of that quick," said Phoebe. "Because we'd better know what we want to do before that potion of yours wears off and all those demons go back to wreaking havoc."

Chapter Eighteen

It was dark. Not only outside, but inside the Manor's kitchen as well. The three sisters sat around the kitchen table, glum. The Book of Shadows lay on the table in front of them. Notes from seven different spells had been added together, amended, crossed out, and then wadded up and trashed. No one had bothered to turn on a light. It was almost as if they hadn't noticed the darkness creeping up on them.

Leo stepped in at the doorway and turned on the overhead lights. Piper shaded her eyes. "Do you have to make everything so *bright*?"

"Sorry." He gave the three of them a moment to adjust to the light. "I take it things haven't gone all that well."

"Wait, where's Chase?" Paige asked Leo.

"Back upstairs."

"Where'd you two go?"

"Hawaii."

Paige nodded. "Was it . . . nice? For him?"

"Very nice. He'd never been before. Always wanted to go there."

Piper frowned. "How could you possibly know that? He still can't speak, can he?"

"No," admitted Leo. "I had some help from the Elders. They sort of scanned him."

"Okay," said Piper, "let's hear it."

"Why do you say it like that?" asked Phoebe. "Maybe he's got good news."

"If it were good news, he would have told us the minute he got here."

"It's not the kind of news you were looking for," Leo said, "but I think it'll help."

All three sisters leaned forward, waiting.

"Okay," said Leo, "here it is. The reason Chase can't move a muscle except for his eyes is that the demon is using his essence, even his muscle control, to power the body duplications." Leo chose his words carefully. "That's why, if Chase were to die, the demon would have no choice but to return to the egg. Without the incantation on the egg's surface, the demon can't exist in our world. And without being invited by a human who recites that incantation, the demon has no host."

"So," Paige began, "If Chase dies . . ."

"The demon dematerializes immediately," said Leo. "All the copies vanish, and the original becomes incorporeal. Then his essence has only one place to go, one place it can survive."

"Back in the egg," said Piper.

Leo nodded.

The four of them were silent for a long moment.

"Well," said Phoebe, "at least we know that if Chase dies, he dies for a good reason."

Piper nodded. "That's something. Not much, but something."

"Anything else in the Book?" Leo asked. "Anything at all?"

"No," said Piper. "Not yet. But I still—" Her ringing cell phone cut her off. She checked the caller ID before answering. "Hey, Darryl." She looked back at the others. "We're on our way." She closed the phone. "Some plainclothes officer who wasn't aware of the stakeout rousted the demon."

"Oh, no," said Phoebe.

Piper looked at Paige. "Can you stay here? Guard the fort?"

Paige nodded. Leo grabbed Piper's and Phoebe's hands, and the three of them orbed out.

Darryl had his cell phone to his ear when they appeared next to him. He jumped, then put the phone away. "I'll never get used to that," he said.

The fading light in the western sky barely illuminated the mini-park, now alive with activity: Paramedics loaded a wounded man into an ambulance; large numbers of police established a perimeter and held back the crowds; helicopters buzzed overhead, some of them police, some news copters.

"What happened?" asked Phoebe.

Darryl sighed. "An off-duty cop, one who didn't know about the stakeout, walked right up and woke your demon before we could stop him." He shook his head. "Every cop on patrol knew about this. I never thought to get a message to those not on duty."

"What happened after he woke up?"

Darryl looked out over the scene. "He went crazy, assaulting the officer, who drew on him. Fired three slugs into him before the perp—I mean, before the demon grabbed the gun away from him. Shot him in the thigh."

Piper winced. "But he'll live, right?"

Darryl shook his head. "It's going to be tough. The slug hit an artery. He's lost a lot of blood."

Darryl watched as a news van pulled up. "When 'officer down' goes out over the system, there's no way to keep it out of the news."

"One thing at a time," said Piper. "Where's the demon?"

"We lost him in all the excitement." Darryl looked at Piper.

"What aren't you telling us?" she asked.

"When you put that one to sleep, the others bedded down as well."

Piper nodded. "I figured they would."

"Even before you told me about the spell, we were tracking three of them. After this one woke up, those three woke too. Now they're converging."

"Where?" Piper asked.

Darryl turned to a map of the city, which was laid out on one of the park's tables. He pointed as he talked. "We had one spotted here, one here, and one here. And now they're all moving . . . this way."

Piper looked at the map, then at the street behind them. "They're coming here. They're gathering right here, in the financial district."

Darryl nodded. "We haven't seen the others yet, but we expect to. When we triangulate the three whose locations we *do* know, it looks like they should all meet here." He pointed to a place on the map at the edge of the district. "In about an hour. It's an old warehouse." He looked at Piper. "And that's not all."

"What else is there?" Piper asked.

"They're all carrying big, mean-looking swords."

Piper looked from the map to Darryl. "Okay," she said. "Thanks. We know what to do." She turned to face Phoebe and Leo. "Let's go."

Back at the Manor, Piper, Leo, Paige, and Phoebe planned while sitting around the kitchen table.

"We have an hour," Piper said. She looked at Paige. "All of the demons are gathering, and they're carrying their decapitation swords."

"So," Paige began, "the destruction and the mayhem that Phoebe envisioned—that all starts about an hour from now."

"Looks that way," Piper said. "Here's what I want. First, we make a last-ditch, if-nothing-else-works plan."

Paige sat back a little in her chair. "You mean a plan where Chase . . ."

"Yes. That's what I mean." She reached for Paige's hand. "But it's only a last resort. Then we spend the rest of our hour finding another way."

"So, in this last-ditch plan," said Phoebe, "who does it?" When no one spoke, she went on. "I mean, does it have to be violent? Can't it be . . . you know . . . merciful?"

"If we turn Chase over to the SWAT team," Leo said, "it probably *will* be violent."

"What if we asked Darryl?" Paige suggested quietly. The others turned toward her, surprised. "I mean—just for this last-ditch thing of yours— Darryl would understand. He could be kind. Chase just went to Hawaii, after all, so if we orb him somewhere nice . . . and Darryl just sort of snuck up behind him . . ."

"He wouldn't even know what hit him," said Phoebe.

Paige nodded.

"Could we ask Darryl to do such a thing?" asked Leo.

"Someone has to do it," said Piper. "We can't do it. If we want to be nice about it, I think we have to ask Darryl. And then we all have to live with it."

They were silent for a moment.

"Okay," said Piper, looking at her watch. "That's our last-ditch plan. Now, on to another plan."

"What plan?" asked Phoebe. "What can we try that we haven't thought of?"

"If you knew that," Leo said matter-of-factly, "then you would have thought of it already."

"Leo," said Piper, slight annoyance creeping into her voice, "no semantic games right now."

"I'm only saying that just because you haven't thought of something doesn't mean there isn't an answer out there."

Piper narrowed her eyes at him. "Leo Wyatt, if you know something that you're not telling us—"

"I don't." Leo raised his hands in a sign of surrender. "Honest." He put one hand on Piper's arm. "But I have faith in you three. I believe there's another answer out there."

"You realize, of course," Piper said, "that if you're wrong, if we can't think of another plan in the next hour, you've just made things that much worse."

"Let's ask for help," said Phoebe. "Let's conjure any witch, living or dead, who might be able to help vanquish these guys."

"Good idea," Paige said.

As Paige and Phoebe drew a circle and lit the candles, Piper wrote on a piece of paper. "I think I can come up with a spell that should work," she said.

"Write a copy for each of us," said Phoebe. "It'll save you the time of having to teach it to us."

"Right," said Piper. "We need all the time we can get."

When she'd finished, the three sisters sat in the circle, each with a copy of the incantation in her lap. They reached out, grasped one another's hands, and began.

> *Kindred spirits, every one, listen to our*
> *call.*
> *Be ye here or be ye gone, we need you, one*
> *and all.*
> *In our presence, be it known, a demon*
> *walks once more.*
> *We seek your help to vanquish it to where*
> *it dwelled before.*
> *If one among you has the means to deal*
> *this fateful blow,*
> *Appear before us, and divulge the secrets*
> *that you know.*

A swirl, like a soft breath of wind, began, slowly circling the three as they sat.

"It's working," Phoebe whispered. "Let's repeat it."

They began the chant again, this time their voices more urgent, more pleading.

> *Kindred spirits, every one, listen to our*
> *call.*
> *Be ye here or be ye gone, we need you, one*
> *and all.*

As they spoke these words, the swirling wind around them gathered speed, increasing in volume. They spoke louder.

> *In our presence, be it known, a demon*
> *walks once more.*
> *We seek your help to vanquish it to where*
> *it dwelled before.*

They had to raise their voices even more to hear one another as they finished the incantation.

> *If one among you has the means to deal*
> *this fateful blow,*
> *Appear before us, and divulge the secrets*
> *that you know.*

The papers inscribed with the incantation lifted off their laps and swirled away. The candles fought the wind, then went out one by one. The three sisters, each with hair flying in her eyes, fought to see.

The winds slowed to a gentle breeze once

more. Hair and paper fluttered back to where they belonged. The candles relit themselves.

A column of swirling light formed in the center of the room, looking like a slow-motion hurricane. In this calmer vortex a woman's likeness appeared, but remained an incorporeal image of herself, barely visible through the soft swirl of light.

"Grams," whispered Piper. "Grams, we need you."

The image of Grams smiled, but it was a sad smile. She shook her head slightly. A single tear ran down her cheek. Her image faded away.

The column of light dispersed. The wind died completely, the flickering candles the only movement now. The house became silent once more. The three of them sat, still holding hands.

"Well," said Phoebe, "that didn't work."

"I think it did, in a way," said Piper. "I think Grams came to tell us that there isn't anyone out there who knows any more about how to stop this demon than we do."

Paige stared at her sullenly. "And how does that help, exactly?"

"Because now we know we've exhausted every other possibility." Piper looked at her watch. "Now we know what we have to do. And we know we have to do it soon."

"Chase can't do anything to get his affairs in order," said Paige. "He can't even tell us who to call, when this is all over."

"We should all go say good-bye," Piper said softly, "and then we should go get Darryl."

Paige took in a sharp breath. "Wait. Can't we . . ." She looked from one sister to the other, trying to find something to hang on to. "Can't we at least put him in some kind of trance? Make sure he can't feel anything?"

"That sounds like the kindest thing to do," said Piper. "Yeah, I think we can do that. I can probably even—" She stopped, looking at her sisters. "Wait a minute. What if we put him in a death trance?"

Phoebe cocked her head. "You mean, like in *Romeo and Juliet*?"

"Yes," said Piper, "exactly." She paused. "What did Leo say?" She turned. "Leo?"

Leo walked in, holding Wyatt.

Piper rose, stepped out of the circle, and crossed to him. "You said something about how Chase is paralyzed because his motor functions are being used by the demon to animate all the doubles."

"Yeah," said Leo, "that's it, basically."

"What if, instead of killing him, we put Chase in a trance that *mimics* death? What happens to that motor control then?"

"Then," said Leo, catching on, "all his motor skills should stop."

Phoebe and Paige rose to join the conversation.

"But if Chase isn't really dead," Phoebe mused, "do all the demons go poof?"

"Maybe not," said Paige, "but if they can't move, they can't very well cause much damage, can they?"

"And while they're looking dead," Piper added, "we find a way to vanquish them. For good."

"Let's do it," said Phoebe. "Right now."

Piper glanced at her watch. "I'll go look up the recipe for the Romeo-and-Juliet potion." She looked at Paige. "Why don't you go explain to Chase, if you can, what we're going to do." She stopped. "I mean, this potion is risky. It could possibly slip into the real thing."

"I understand," said Paige. "I'll make sure he does too."

"Speaking of making sure, make sure we have his permission," said Piper. "This might not work without it."

The three sisters went up to the attic. Piper looked through the Book while Phoebe and Paige talked to Chase. Piper could barely make out what they were saying as she turned pages, looking for the instruction she remembered. She found it.

To pattern death in every way,
In breath, in heart, in soul,
To bring a loved one to the point
Where even skin grows cold,
Then mark ye well the potion
Which on these pages lies,

From sun to sun, or moon to moon,
The one who drinks it, dies.

Piper looked up from the Book. "Paige?"

Paige, kneeling over Chase, her face close to his, lifted her head and looked at Piper. "He's ready."

"This is for a loved one. So . . . do you love him?"

Paige glanced down at Chase once more, then looked back at Piper, nodding. "Yeah. I guess I do."

"Good enough." Piper copied the ingredients for the potion. "Phoebe? What time does the moon rise tonight?"

Phoebe checked the lunar calendar hanging on the wall. "In . . . fourteen minutes." She looked back at Piper. "How did you know?"

"I didn't." Piper finished the list. "But I think our luck is beginning to change."

Working in the kitchen, Piper silently thanked Grams for teaching her to always keep her herb drawers well stocked. She finished brewing the potion in about ten minutes.

She brought the steaming broth up to the attic and handed it to Paige. "You should be the one to give it to him," she said. She knelt by Chase. "Don't be afraid. If this goes well, you'll be back to normal this time tomorrow."

Chase blinked twice.

Paige spooned a bit of the broth into his

mouth, gently stroking his throat until he swallowed. She spooned in a little more.

Piper glanced at Phoebe, then looked at her
watch. She rose, crossed to the window, and
looked out. A glow above the trees showed where
the moon was about to rise. "Paige? Hurry if you
can."

Paige nodded, keeping her concentration on
Chase.

Piper watched as a sliver of the moon began
to emerge. "So when exactly is moonrise? From
the first moment we see it, or after it's all the
way up?"

She heard the spoon clatter to the floor
behind her, and turned.

Paige kneeled, stroking Chase's head. "Chase?
Chase?" Her hand went to her mouth. "Oh, he
looks so . . ."

Piper crossed to the cot and knelt down next
to Paige. "Yes," she agreed, "he looks dead." She
reached over and closed his lifeless eyes. "But
that was the plan."

Paige nodded. "I know. But seeing it up
close . . ."

"Yeah." Piper put her arm around her sister.
"From moon to moon. That's how much time
we've got. Let's make the most of it."

Paige nodded.

Piper pulled out her cell phone and punched
in Darryl's number. "Hey, Darryl, it's Piper.
How many officers are with you, tracking the

demons?" She nodded. "Just the three of you? Can you pull them back?" She looked at her sisters. "I don't know, tell them anything you want. . . ."

Phoebe stepped closer to Piper. "Tell him to say that they can't risk being seen. Tell him they're going to wait for the gang's next move."

Piper repeated Phoebe's instructions, then added, "We're on our way." She closed the phone and turned to her sisters. "Let's go."

Chapter Nineteen

The three sisters orbed into the abandoned warehouse.

Phoebe looked around. "This is kind of creepy."

"It's not creepy, Phoebe, it's just old."

"No, I meant that this is ground zero for the demons' plan to lay waste to our city."

"Oh. That." Piper strained to see better in the dark. The moonlight coming in at the windows helped. She began to make out the design of the structure.

They were in a row of gutted offices. An open door in front of them led to the main portion of the warehouse. Piper pointed to the door. "I think this will lead us to the spot where Darryl said they're all converging." She walked toward the door. "Let's find our boys."

Phoebe walked beside her. "You mean our ghouls?"

Piper looked at her, surprised.

"Don't worry," said Phoebe, "that's just nerves."

"Really?" asked Paige. "I thought it was a corny pun."

They stepped through the door into the warehouse, which stretched high and wide, as cavernous as an aircraft hangar.

In the moonlight, a single demon moved while all the other demons lay prostrate on the floor. Still holding his sword, the mobile demon slowly worked his way from inert body to inert body.

"He must be the original," said Paige softly. "I thought this would have worked on him, too."

"So did I," said Piper.

The demon turned toward them, glowering. He staggered on his feet, raising his sword. "You . . . ," he muttered.

"He looks almost down for the count too," whispered Phoebe. "Maybe we should, you know, engage him, wear him down further."

Piper nodded, stepping forward to address the demon directly. "That's right, us. We're the ones who crashed your little party."

The demon lurched forward and she reflexively raised her hands, ready to blow him across the room, but he staggered, stopped, and dropped the point of his sword to the ground, apparently too weak to hold it up anymore.

"It's over," said Piper. "Why don't you go

back in your little egg and hole up for another couple of millennia?"

The demon's head sagged, then rose off his chest. "My host . . ." He looked down at his body, then at the copies of Chase lying motionless across the floor. He cocked his head, seeming to gather what strength he had left. "My host . . . ," he repeated, ". . . is not dead." A gleam came into his eye.

"He's onto us," said Paige. "He knows."

Piper nodded. "If the real Chase were dead, none of them would be here. He's got that much figured out."

The demon lifted the sword, mustering what strength he had left. "My host," he said again, "is not dead. But not alive." He moved to the closest clone, raised the sword, and plunged it into the body. The body lurched, then exploded into a mist, which the demon absorbed. He walked to the next body, becoming stronger, slamming the sword home and absorbing the vapors that burst forth. As he worked, he muttered, "This . . . is . . . not . . . acceptable."

"What?" asked Paige, watching. "Limp bodies aren't acceptable, so he's doing our work for us?"

"Somehow I don't think this is a good thing," Piper replied.

The monster slashed the next bodies two at a time, moving faster as the mist of all the bodies swirled around, consolidating into him.

"He's absorbing them," said Phoebe. "He's

merging back to one. And he's getting stronger while he's doing it."

"Stop him," said Paige.

"How?" asked Piper.

"Freeze him!"

Piper gestured and the demon froze, the blade of his sword inches from another body.

The Charmed Ones breathed a collective sigh of relief.

"What is going on?" asked Phoebe. "First, he shouldn't be up and around at all."

"I'm not sure why he's mobile," said Piper, "but it's pretty obvious that his strength is spread over all the copies. The fewer copies, the stronger he is."

"How many did he absorb?" asked Phoebe.

Paige counted. "Eight."

Phoebe stared at the demon, her eyes going wide. "Piper . . . ?"

Piper looked to where Phoebe was staring.

From the body closest to the frozen demon a mist appeared, rising slowly only inches away from the tip of the demon's sword. The body began to disintegrate, and the demon's blade sucked up the mist as if the sword were a vacuum cleaner, until the vapor and the body were both gone.

Phoebe squinted. "Is he . . . moving?" The three sisters stepped closer.

Slowly, so slowly that it was barely noticeable, the demon moved toward the next body.

"Why isn't your freeze holding?" asked Paige.

Piper shook her head. "Maybe because it was part of what killed him at the clock tower. Maybe because he's just too powerful." She looked at her sisters. "But freezing was only a temporary reprieve, anyway. We've got to get him back in that egg."

"Look," said Paige. "I know he's getting stronger, but maybe we should let him absorb all of them."

Piper looked at her, incredulous. "Why?"

"So we only have one to deal with."

"I say we get rid of him now," said Piper, "then come back for the rest of the inert ones."

"Okay," said Paige, "but remember, we only have until the moon rises again. Then they're all active once more."

"While you two are arguing," said Phoebe, "he's sucking up another one."

Piper looked over. Sure enough, the demon had managed to point his sword at the next body, and even from several feet away he was absorbing the life force back into himself.

"This ends here. And now," said Piper. She gestured at the demon, intending to blow him into pieces. Instead, she hurled him across the warehouse so that he smashed into the wall. The demon, obviously dead, fell and split into two.

"Oops," said Phoebe.

"No, look," said Paige.

One of the demons rose, but the other lay inert, like the rest of the copies.

"Enough!" roared the demon. With one gesture he vaporized all the remaining bodies, taking up their essence into himself.

"Okay, end of discussion," said Piper. "Now we deal with one."

"Careful," Phoebe said. "I think he just got a lot stronger."

The demon raised his blade and rushed at Phoebe, bellowing, blade held back, ready to decapitate her.

Piper gestured and hurled him into the wall, but this time he bounced off, regained his balance, and came roaring at Phoebe again. His sword was raised behind his shoulder, prepared to deliver a killing blow.

Piper gestured again, and this time the demon only staggered back a step or two. He smiled, raised his sword, and charged a third time.

"That's it," said Paige, grabbing her sisters' hands. "Retreat." She orbed them out just before the blade swung home.

The sisters appeared outside the warehouse. "Thanks," said Phoebe. "That was pretty close."

"Here he comes," said Piper.

They watched as the demon emerged from the warehouse. He turned slowly in a circle, sniffing the air, then headed off in a particular direction.

"He's going somewhere specific," said Piper.

"Let's follow," Paige suggested.

The demon moved fast. His long, powerful legs quickly strode over the ground. The sisters had trouble keeping up.

They followed for several blocks, Piper urging them faster whenever they lagged more than a hundred yards behind. They were beginning to tire.

"I don't . . . think he's . . . looking to cause any destruction right now," said Piper, panting as she talked.

"No," agreed Paige. "He's making a . . . beeline somewhere."

Phoebe stopped.

"Come on, Phoebes," said Paige. "No time to rest now."

"I think I know where he's going," said Phoebe.

Piper and Paige immediately halted. The demon quickly increased the distance between them.

"Where?" Piper asked.

"Look at where we started. Look at where we are. Draw a straight line and keep going, and in another few miles we'll be at—"

"The Manor," Piper said.

"He's sensing something," Paige guessed. "The egg?"

"I don't think so," said Piper. She looked ahead at the demon, nearly out of sight. "We've got to keep up."

They broke into a run, continuing until they were within twenty-five yards of the demon, who didn't look back but simply kept his long, purposeful stride.

"I don't think he's after the egg," said Piper, puffing harder now. "The egg does him no good. He's here to destroy civilization as we know it. He must be—"

"After Chase," Paige and Phoebe said in unison, working to keep up.

"But why?" asked Piper.

Phoebe stopped again. "Wait."

Paige grabbed her arm. "You can't stop every time you have an idea—he's going to get away."

"Remember what he said when he was zapping all the other bodies?" Phoebe asked.

"He said, 'This is not acceptable,'" Piper replied.

"Yes," said Phoebe, "and we thought he was talking about the bodies being nothing but lumps as being not acceptable. We thought that's why he reabsorbed them all. But what if that's not what he meant?"

Piper looked at Phoebe while still moving quickly ahead. "Yes! Because just before that, he'd said something about his host being not dead but not alive. If that's what he meant when he said 'not acceptable,' then he can't allow Chase to be in limbo. He has to be one way or the other." The thought hit home. "He's out to kill Chase."

"We could orb back to the Manor," said Phoebe, "get Chase out of there."

Piper shook her head. "And leave the Manor to Mr. Destruction? I don't think so." She stopped, watching the demon disappear in front of them. Her sisters stopped too. "We can't fight him like this," she said. "Look at us. We can barely catch our breath, and he hasn't even broken stride." She turned to Paige. "Orb us in front of him."

"And then what?" asked Paige.

"Then we take him on," said Piper. "Then we stop him."

"How?" asked Phoebe. "We can't stab him, shoot him, freeze him, blow him up, run him over with a car, or throw him off a building. What's left?"

"Orb us in front of him," said Piper. "I've got an idea."

Paige orbed them twenty yards in front of the demon, who stopped. "You again," he growled, raising his sword. He began to walk forward.

Piper gestured, freezing him.

"What are you doing?" asked Phoebe. "We know this won't work. Look, he's still moving."

"Yes," agreed Piper, "but very slowly. Kick him, Phoebe. Give him your best karate move. See if you can knock his head off."

"Okay," said Phoebe. She ran at him, delivering a flying roundhouse kick. Her foot landed squarely across his head, knocking it sharply to the side. She came down hobbling. "Owwww," she said. "That's like kicking a statue."

"Sorry." Piper unfroze the demon, and he slumped to the sidewalk. "You did it, though. See? His neck's broken."

"I don't get this," said Phoebe, rubbing her foot. "Now he'll just split in two."

"Yes," said Piper, "and while he's splitting, he's vulnerable. Besides, if we keep him from absorbing inert body number two, he'll be weaker."

"Got it," said Paige. "I'll orb the inert bodies back to the warehouse."

As they watched, the heap on the sidewalk became two demons. A taxi rolled by, too far from them for the passengers to see what was going on. "Good thing most people are too scared to be out tonight," said Piper.

One of the demons began to move. Paige quickly orbed away with the other.

"Come on," said Piper. "Let's take cover. Let him start for the Manor again." They did.

The demon stood, cleared his head, and began to walk again. After a moment, Piper and Phoebe followed.

"See?" said Piper. "He's walking slower now."

"Good thing," said Phoebe, limping beside her. "I think I broke my foot."

Paige orbed back beside them, carrying a crossbow.

"Where did you get that?" Piper asked.

"Sporting goods store," said Paige. She took

aim and fired a bolt into the demon. Once again, he slumped to the sidewalk.

The sisters hurried to catch up to him before he finished splitting. Again, Paige orbed away with the motionless body.

Phoebe sat down, rubbing her foot. "He looks more like Chase now, not as hunky as he was."

"You're right," said Piper. "This might be working."

Paige orbed back with a diver's speargun.

"Same store?" Phoebe asked.

Paige nodded and fired the gun at the demon. This time, he merely pulled out the spear and kept walking.

"Too similar," said Paige. "I should have known."

"We've got to dilute him further," said Phoebe, still hobbling.

"Poison?" asked Paige.

"I don't know where we'd find any over-the-counter stuff," said Piper, "and we don't have time to make any of our own."

"We're only a few blocks from home," said Phoebe. "Look, back at that warehouse he could barely stand when he was split over all the demons. Right now he looks to be about half as strong as he was at his best, when he left the warehouse. So if we can hit him one more time, I think we'll be dealing with a demon at one quarter power."

"I could drop him off the Golden Gate Bridge,"

said Paige. "I don't think he's drowned yet."

"But then we'd lose track of him," said Piper, "and we can't risk not knowing where he'll be at moonrise tomorrow."

"He's turning down our street," said Paige. "Whatever we do, it's got to be now."

"Get to the attic," said Piper, "and be ready to orb Chase out of there."

"What are you two going to do?" Paige asked.

"I don't know yet," said Piper. "I'm still thinking."

"Okay." Paige didn't look convinced, but she orbed away.

"What *are* you going to do?" asked Phoebe. "He's crossing into our backyard."

Piper turned to her. "I need your strength, Phoebes. I need you to channel your energy into me. Maybe the two of us together can knock him down again, can reduce him by half again."

"Worth a try," said Phoebe. She closed her eyes, laid her hands on Piper's shoulders, and concentrated.

Piper put one hand over Phoebe's, then, mustering all the power she could, she shot a bolt of energy at the demon.

It did indeed knock him off his feet, sending his sword flying. He lay motionless in their yard.

Piper ran up, Phoebe hobbling beside her. "Would beheading him with his own sword be different from the ways he's been killed before?" Piper asked.

Phoebe picked up the sword, handing it to Piper. "Go for it," she said.

Piper raised the blade and brought it down with all her strength at the demon's neck.

Quick as a flash, the demon grabbed the blade with one hand, his fingers impervious to the razor-sharp steel. With his other hand he grabbed Piper's wrist, twisted her around, and brought the blade up under her neck. He looked at Phoebe. "Tell the one who can fly to bring me the host," he said, "and the egg. Or I slit this one's throat."

Phoebe stared, horrified at the sight of the demon on the ground, Piper frightened and in his grasp on top of him. "Paige, we need you," she said softly.

Paige orbed in beside her, laying Chase on the ground as she did. "I heard," she said. She set the two halves of the egg down and stood over Chase protectively. "Let her go first."

"No," said the demon.

"Then we've got no deal," said Paige. "Because we sure aren't going to trust you."

"So be it. She dies," said the demon. He moved the blade slightly, and a small red gash opened on Piper's neck.

"Wait!" cried Phoebe. "Tell us how you want to do this."

The demon struggled to get to his feet, still

keeping the blade on Piper's neck, which now bled severely. "I take his essence, as I did that of my fallen comrades. When I have it, I will once again become mist myself, and go back into the egg. Your sister will then be free."

Paige stood openmouthed, trying to think of any way out of this.

The demon drew the blade across Piper's neck again, opening the cut further. "Do not look for a way to defeat me. I will kill her. Release him to me now!"

"All right!" Paige stepped back.

As soon as she did, the demon pointed the sword at Chase and turned into a mist, the sword clattering to the ground.

The second that Piper was free of him, she turned, gesturing toward the tendril of mist that headed for the egg. It exploded into a thousand tiny fireworks, like sparklers, which all went out in an instant.

The egg crumbled to dust.

"Chase!" Paige screamed. She dropped to his side, scooping him into her lap, cradling him. "Chase! I'm so sorry!" She looked up, tears steaming down her face. "I'm taking him back to the attic." She orbed him away.

Phoebe stepped to Piper, looking at her neck. "This is serious."

"I don't think so," she said. "If he'd done any lethal damage, there'd be a lot more blood."

"How did you destroy him?" Phoebe asked.

"First, I was really, really angry," said Piper. "And, when you and I had channeled together, it helped. So I knew, even without asking, that if I could channel all three of us, I could end him. Especially when he was no longer in his body." She held her hand over her neck, trying to slow the bleeding. "I just wish we could've saved Chase, too."

"Let's get you to a doctor," said Phoebe. "I'm sure you're going to need stitches."

Chapter Twenty

The sky was becoming light when Phoebe and Piper returned from the emergency room. Phoebe wore a plastic boot on her foot and walked on crutches. Piper had a large gauze bandage covering the gash on her neck.

They made their way to the attic.

Paige sat next to Chase's body, buttoning up a clean shirt. She turned when her sisters came in, sighing the sigh of someone who's been crying. "How are you?" she asked Piper, wiping her eyes.

"Fine," Piper said. "The doctor said I was lucky."

"Twenty-two stitches," said Phoebe. "Another quarter inch deeper and she would have bled to death." She maneuvered to Paige, set the crutches down, and knelt beside her, taking her hands. "You did what you had to. If you had waited another second, he would have killed her."

Paige nodded, fighting the urge to cry again. "How's your foot?"

"She tore some ligaments," said Piper. "Has to stay off it for a while."

"Look at us," said Paige glumly. "Some Charmed Ones."

"We know what would have happened if we'd let him go," said Piper. "Phoebe saw it."

"And," said Phoebe, "thanks to Piper, he's never going to come back and do that to civilization again. Ever."

"Thanks to all of us," said Piper. "I wouldn't have had the strength without you two."

Paige nodded, considering this. "Like the Book says, we have to count the greater good. I just wish . . ." Her tears started again. She buried her face in her hands.

Phoebe reached out and enfolded her sister in her arms.

Piper walked over to join them, putting her arms around them both. She looked over at Chase. "I see you've shaved him."

Paige nodded. "And combed his hair, gave it a trim." She fingered the shirt. "I hope you don't mind," she said to Piper. "This is one of Leo's."

"No," said Piper. "He looks good in it."

Paige looked up. "I thought he should look his best when we send him back to his family."

"How'd you find them?" asked Phoebe.

"His Kansas driver's license. I tracked him

the way we did at social services when . . . when
something like this happened."

Piper sighed. "He looks so peaceful. Just like
he did in the—" She stopped.

"The death trance," said Phoebe, picking up
on Piper's meaning. "Do you think it could have
protected him?"

Paige looked up, her eyes darting from Piper
to Phoebe. "What? Protected him?"

Piper nodded. "When the demon was harvesting the essence of all his doubles, we saw a
mist rise up from each of them, and join him."

"Right," Phoebe said excitedly. "But when he
pointed his sword at Chase, nothing happened
except that *he* turned into mist."

"So you . . ." Paige could hardly bring herself
to hope. "You think Chase is still in the trance?"

"Only one way to find out," said Piper.

The three sisters sat in the dim light of the attic,
candles lit around Chase's deathly form. For the
third time in two minutes, Paige rose and walked
to the window, waiting for the moon to rise.
"This is killing me," she said. "I mean, what if—"

"Don't think like that," said Phoebe. "In fact,
try not to think at all."

Paige paced back to the cot and sat beside
Chase, smoothing a lock of his hair back into
place.

"Paige?" Piper nodded to the window, where
the first glimmer of the rising moon filtered in.

At that instant, Chase took in a breath, his eyes fluttered open, and he focused on Paige. "Hey," he said softly. "It worked."

"Chase!" Paige reached out, placing a hand on each side of his face, then hugged him tight. "Are you all right?"

"I think so." He tried to sit up. "Whoa," he said. "Nothing seems to be working quite right."

"That's probably because your muscles haven't been working at all for almost a week now," said Piper. "Take it easy, give it some time."

Chase sat up on the bed, still shaky. He looked over at Phoebe's crutches, at Piper's bandaged neck. "What happened to you two? You look like you were in a war or something."

"Or something," said Paige. "It *was* a war. But our side won."

The story Piper constructed for Darryl didn't satisfy everybody, but it was the story that became official.

While Chase recovered his motor skills, Piper made a plaster mold of his face and fashioned a dozen formfitting rubber headpieces from it. She gave them to Darryl, who went before the press to announce that the crime spree had been perpetrated by a band of thieves who all dressed alike, wore identical masks, and replaced their fallen comrades with more doubles in order to hide their number and appear invincible. Chase, in Piper's version of the story, was simply the wrong-place, wrong-time museum worker who was kidnapped so that his face could be copied.

Even though Darryl faltered at several of the questions the press threw at him, the story stuck. Mainly, as Piper said, because no one could come up with a better one.

It was a cloudy, blustery day, much like the first day they met, when Chase and Paige walked out along Land's End again.

"You doing okay?" Paige asked. "You're not getting too tired, are you?"

"Nah. I'm fine. Really." He reached for her hand. "You know, when I was lying there, all that time, helpless, I couldn't have asked for any better care than what you gave me. I have to say, watching the way you did what you did, I have never seen anyone who looked so beautiful."

Paige smiled, tucking her hair behind her ear. "Wow. A witch *and* beautiful."

They arrived at the lookout. Paige stared out at the bridge, at the land, at the Pacific as it rolled slowly toward them. "You know," she began, "there are powers in this world, powers that most people don't ever notice." She turned to him. "Just like most tourists don't ever consider the power of the ocean—as you did that first day—most people also don't consider the powers that roam this Earth, for good and for evil. But they're there just the same."

Chase nodded. "I get that now."

Paige snickered. "Well, you'd have to, having your face rubbed in it like you did."

"Yeah."

"I guess," she continued, "my point is, now that you do know, what do you think? I mean, besides the fact that I make a good nurse."

Chase looked a bit uncomfortable. "What are you asking, exactly?"

Paige gazed out at the sea again. "You and I didn't get the chance to, you know, date. Not really. Instead, we got thrust into this. Like we were stuck in the same foxhole or something." She looked back at him. "So, now that you know about me—about my sisters and what we do . . . and you know, because I had to blurt it out in front of you and everyone, that I love you . . ."

Chase watched her, studying her face. "If you're asking what I think about you three, I think you are the strongest ladies I've ever met. I think what you did—what you do—is amazing."

She smiled. "Thanks. But what about that other part? That 'I love you' part?"

"That is really . . . that really means a lot to me." He looked away. "But I'm not that strong."

Paige blinked, looking as if she'd just been pushed off balance. "What . . . ?"

He turned back to her, taking both her hands. "I'd love to get to know you better. Love to pay more attention to the part of me that loves you, too. I'd even want to take you back to meet Mom and Dad, if you were normal. But . . ."

She stiffened. "But I'm not. Normal. I'm the freak who saved you." She tried to smile, as if this were a joke, but it tightened up on her. "I get it."

"Paige, please understand. I mean, right now, looking at you, thinking about how good you were to me . . . if I didn't know the rest of it, I'd want you to be mine. No question."

She pushed her hair back off her face, turning to the sea, turning away from his gaze. "I know it's a lot to ask, to take on who we are. I was just thinking how great it would be to have a man in my life who understood, who I didn't have to lie to. Who could treat me as if I were . . . you know . . . normal."

"Yeah. I can see that. And that's exactly what you deserve. But that's not me."

Paige nodded, staring out at the ocean, a numbness creeping into her. "So," she managed, "what about all that stuff you know now? About me and my sisters, I mean."

"I won't say a word to anybody. Promise. I owe you at least that much." He smiled. "Who'd believe a story like that, anyway?"

Paige tried to smile back, but it didn't take. "What *will* you tell people?"

He looked up, thinking. "I came to San Francisco, met you, worked in the museum, got kidnapped by the gang, was held in a dark closet where I knew nothing, not even how many days had gone by, until I was rescued."

She nodded. She saw a bus pull up in front of

the museum and recognized it as the same tour operator that had brought Chase here in the first place. She caught on. "And now you've brought me here so you can say good-bye?"

"Yeah."

A blast of wind swept over them. He turned to the ocean, opening his coat to the gust, greeting it as he had on his first day in town. But this time, instead of embracing the wind, Chase wrapped his coat back around himself. "Whoa," he said, "the Pacific feels a lot colder today."

"Yeah. Those unseen forces at work."

He shivered, then looked at Paige. "You see? That's why I'm not the guy for you. I'd always be trying to guess whether Mother Nature just did that, or you."

Paige looked into those clear, sea green eyes for the last time. "I understand."

"Good."

The bus at the museum honked its horn.

Chase looked over, then looked back. "Well, that's my ride." He leaned over, kissing her softly on her cheek. "Thanks, Paige, for everything." He smiled. "And thanks for all the Greek lessons."

Despite her sorrow, Paige laughed. "You're welcome."

"Gotta go." He stepped back, watching her, then turned and ran for the bus.

Paige looked back at the ocean. She couldn't

stand to see the bus leave and was determined not to shed any more tears.

She was nearly successful.

Piper, Phoebe, and Paige sat around the dining table at the Manor.

"That little creep said *what*? After all you did for him?"

"Relax, Phoebe," said Paige. "It's okay. Like you always say, these things happen for a reason."

"You saved his *life*," said Phoebe. "At least twice."

"Look, it's not easy to accept who we are."

Phoebe sighed. "I guess."

"I think you're right," said Piper, who held Wyatt in her lap. "I do think this is for the best. Still, it's got to hurt."

Paige nodded.

"I'm really sorry," Piper added. "After all you did, because you loved him, hurting you just doesn't seem fair."

Phoebe leaned over, pressing her hand over Paige's. "Are you sure you're okay?"

"No. But I will be. I *am* sure of that."

"Leo?" Piper called. When he came into the room, she handed Wyatt over. "Watch our little slugger for a while, will you? We three are going out for ice cream."

Phoebe nodded, pulling Paige up out of her chair. "Good idea. The biggest, best-tasting, most decadent ice-cream sundae we can find."

Paige smiled sadly. "Thanks, that does sound good."

"Ice cream can't fix everything," said Phoebe, "but it sure comes close." She stopped. "Did I just sound like I was answering an 'Ask Phoebe' letter?"

Paige and Piper both laughed. The three sisters headed for the door, their arms around one another.

"We're the protectors of the innocent.
We're known as the Charmed Ones."

–Phoebe Halliwell, "Something Wiccan This Way Comes"

Go behind the scenes of television's sexiest
supernatural thriller with *The Book of Three*, the
only fully authorized companion to the witty,
witchy world of *Charmed*!

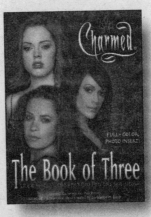

"We all need to believe that magic exists."
–Phoebe Halliwell, "Trial by Magic"

When Phoebe Halliwell returned to San Francisco to live with her older sisters, Prue and Piper, in Halliwell Manor, she had no idea the turn her life—*all* their lives—would take. Because when Phoebe found the Book of Shadows in the Manor's attic, she learned that she and her sisters were the Charmed Ones, the most powerful witches of all time. Battling demons, warlocks, and other black-magic baddies, Piper and Phoebe lost Prue but discovered their long-lost half-Whitelighter, half-witch sister, Paige Matthews. The Power of Three was reborn.

Look for a new Charmed novel every other month!

Published by Simon & Schuster

As many as 1 in 3 Americans
who have HIV... don't know it.

TAKE CONTROL.
KNOW YOUR STATUS.
GET TESTED.

To learn more about HIV testing,
or get a free guide to HIV and
other sexually transmitted diseases:

www.knowhivaids.org
1-866-344-KNOW